A REBEL'S TRUST

Alaskan Rebels

Book 4

SARA BLACKARD

Chapter One

Sunny Rebel meticulously checked through her supplies spread out on her old bed in her parents' house against the list she'd made as Otis Redding softly crooned to her from her portable speaker. In the morning, she would leave for her next solo adventure, a trek through the Fortymile Mining District north of Chicken in the Alaskan Interior. Getting all the gear organized and accounted for meant less chance of mishap on the trail. Not that a well-stocked pack could prevent disaster from striking. She'd just be better prepared if it did.

"All right, folks." She looked into her phone's camera as she finished up her live feed to her social media accounts. "I think I have everything I need." She paused and leaned close, like she wanted to tell a secret. "Don't tell anyone about the LemonHead candies. They aren't a necessity, but I figure they're not that heavy." Laughing emojis filled her screen as she pasted on a smile and straightened. "I can't wait to get back and show you my adventures in Alaskan gold country!"

She chuckled as heart and thumbs up emojis

exploded on her screen from people hitting their love and like buttons. Sure, it wasn't like getting a real hug or high five, but it would do. Her growing list of fans kept her going when the loneliness of solo adventuring sunk in.

"And if you are the praying sort, send a few up for the bears to stay far away." She pushed her lips to one side and lifted a dark eyebrow, amazed at how comfortable she'd become at seeing herself on the screen. "Now, if you are the type of person who enjoys terrifying danger, please remember that all I have for protection is that pea-shooter and a couple handfuls of bullets to keep me safe when you hope for the opposite." Laughing emojis filled her screen again, and she wrinkled her nose at the amount. "Well, unless something goes wrong, I'll see you in a few weeks. Now, go find yourself an adventure!"

She waved and signed off. Her smile fell with a sigh as comments flooded in about viewers wishing they could come with her. Honestly, she wished the same. Being alone weighed on her. At some point, when she had more money, should she think about taking others on the trips? It would increase her income, and, with the way her followers kept growing, she could probably charge a decent guiding fee.

When she'd started the YouTube channel, it had been a knee-jerk reaction to her business partner/boyfriend stealing all their funds and gear from their Denali guiding business and leaving the country. His duplicity had left her broke, both in money and in her heart. She couldn't take climbers up Mount Denali if she didn't have the cash for the gear necessary for the trek up America's highest peak. She definitely didn't want to jump into another venture without being the one in control.

Her phone pinged, pulling her from a spiral into a pity party that included her downing a carton of Moose Tracks ice cream and crying over some sappy movie. A message notification from her climbing friend, Izzy. Wasn't she on Everest this season?

Sunny swiped her phone and opened the message.

Izzy: You'll never guess who I just saw.

Sunny: Sgeti the Yeti?

Izzy: No. Jed. He was feeding breakfast sausages to Marcy Ansley like she couldn't use her own hands. Do you remember her from that time we climbed Annapurna that one summer?

Sunny: Good for them.

Izzy: Yeah, I guess they are taking climbers up this summer. If I didn't have a conscience, I'd totally be sabotaging their gear. I can't believe he has the nerve to show up here, and with her! Makes me so mad. Total jerkface. I was tempted to throat punch him for you.

Sunny: He's not worth the effort. Listen, I have to go. Be safe up there.

Izzy: You too! I miss you. When I get back to the states this fall, we are totally hanging out.

Sunny: Can't wait.

Sunny tapped the Do Not Disturb icon on her phone and tossed it onto the bed. So, Jed crawled out from whatever rock he'd spent the winter hiding under? And with Marcy? Sunny closed her eyes to the sting of tears. She wanted to be furious. Only, she couldn't help but think how similar she and Marcy were.

Both happy-go-lucky.

Quick to trust.

Naïve.

Well, Sunny wasn't a gullible sap anymore. She'd learned the lesson that she couldn't rely on anyone but herself and her family. So, sticking with filming her solo trips in hopes her social media would generate enough income to live on still was her best option.

"Knock, knock." Her mom came into the room carrying two steaming mugs. "I thought you could use some hot chocolate while you finished packing."

Sunny blinked her tears away and smiled. "Your hot chocolate is exactly what I need right now."

Mom's forehead furrowed as she handed the mug to Sunny. "Everything okay?"

"Yeppers." Sunny forced the hurt down, hopefully far enough that her mom would buy it. "Just finished my last live video before I leave, and now I need to get everything packed up."

"Hmm." Mom sipped her drink. The look she gave Sunny fairly screamed she hadn't hidden her emotions well enough.

Darn her mom and her superhuman powers. Maybe it was because Sunny was the youngest of the seven Rebel siblings, and Mom had lots of practice before Sunny arrived, but she could never hide her feelings growing up. Looked like she had gotten no better as an adult.

"You know, honey, it's still not too late to change course and get back on the mountain. Your dad said he overheard you talking to an outfitter on Denali who needs you to guide for them." Mom set her mug on the dresser and placed Sunny's rolled shirts in the ziplock bag draped over her meager clothes.

At least if Mom was going to interrogate her, Sunny appreciated the help while the questions peppered her way. She took a drink of the cinnamony chocolate and tried to let the silky warmth soothe her nerves. When Jed had swindled her out of everything, she hadn't told her family the extent of the betrayal. One, she was afraid her commando brothers and sister Lena would really hunt Jed down like they suggested. She'd barely told them the truth, and they flipped. And, two, her embarrassment over the depth of her involvement with Jed and how she'd put everything she had into the business account was too great to tell anyone ... ever.

"Mom, I like what I'm doing right now." Sunny grabbed the ziplock bag from her mom and placed it in the bottom of her pack. "I'm having fun, and the viewers like it. Besides, I think if I can continue to gain subscribers, I can make a business out of this. Maybe find sponsors or, later, even guide others on adventures with me."

"But I thought you loved climbing Denali." Mom handed her the BushBuddy stove Sunny's friend had given her.

"I did, still do, but I'm ready for something different now."

Was she, though? The call from her outfitter friend

had made her question whether she should just drop this entire solo thing and go back to the mountain she loved. Helping others reach the summit, attempting to conquer one of the world's most treacherous mountains, always thrilled her. Plus, she missed the community, both at base camp and the type of people she used to guide. People who loved the strenuous sport of mountaineering like she did were few and far between. The sense of family and bond created in the endeavor couldn't compare to anything else she'd ever done.

Sunny snatched the food supply pouches and shoved them into her pack. There was no going back for her, at least not yet. She just had to stay her course, no matter how lonely it made her. Maybe then she'd get over her naïve disposition and grow up.

Life hurt, and she couldn't rely on people. Expecting anything else would only prove her ignorance.

Chapter Two

Davis Fields stared out the cabin's only window as he waited for the computer call to connect. He could barely see the tips of the black spruce that circled the remote Alaskan gold camp through the layers of dust on the single pane of glass. At least it wasn't raining. The sun still hid behind the low clouds, but the break in what had been constant drizzle the last week gave Davis hope the call would go through.

The screen flickered, and Rafe Malone, Davis's best friend and now brother-in-law, filled the screen. "Well, if it isn't Paul Bunyan taking time from his busy schedule to call us little people."

"Paul Bunyan was a lumberjack, you twit." Davis rubbed his hand over his beard then through his hair he'd let get scruffy. He hadn't worried about his appearance since he came to the mine. He kind of did resemble Paul Bunyan.

Davis scowled at the computer, but the ribbing settled in his heart.

Rafe was family. Had been since middle school when

Davis's parents died and he and his sister, Piper, moved in with his aunt and uncle. Bouncing meaningless insults back and forth had always been Davis and Rafe's relationship. Rafe was the joker of their duo. Davis, the serious one.

"When is the call of the wild going to stop calling, man? Your sister misses you." Rafe ran his hand over his red hair as he settled into the chair. "I don't. Not one bit. It's not like I'm crying myself to sleep every night because you aren't here to beat at *Mario Kart*."

"Don't know." Davis rolled his eyes. In truth, he wondered if his escape to the Alaskan wilderness was even helping his PTSD.

When his military buddy Justin had said he could use a hand at his gold mine the fall before, Davis had taken the opportunity as a sign. He could spend the spring and summer helping a friend far away from everyone and get a handle on his burning anger and paranoia that simmered just under the surface. Anger sparked by lies and disloyalty during his last deployment. Paranoia leftover from the need to always watch his back. Only problem was being hundreds of miles away from civilization hadn't cooled him down, just left him lonely and frustrated.

Not a good combination.

"Listen—" Rafe sighed and leaned toward the screen. "I know something happened that you aren't telling us about. I've been patient and haven't hacked into the military records to see what it is. But you have to talk to someone, man. Hiding away won't fix things. Trust me. I know."

"What are you talking about?" Davis didn't want to have this conversation.

"I might not have literally run and hid like you, but I hid behind a mask, acting like everything was all right. It took your sister calling me out to make me realize that the more I pushed down my past, the worse I got." Rafe shook his head. "If you can't talk to me, talk to someone. Every single one of us here at Stryker understands on some level what you're going through, man. We all want you to find healing so you can move on, find a beautiful woman to marry, and have wonderful babies. My boys need cousins."

"Moving a little fast, don't you think?"

Davis wanted that. In fact, he'd met someone at his friend Lena Rebel's wedding last fall that he'd been comfortable around. But he couldn't get into a relationship when he felt at any minute he'd blow. He wouldn't physically hurt her, but he couldn't guarantee a verbal outburst wouldn't bruise or crush. But his reaction to her had given him enough hope he could get a handle on his PTSD, so he'd hauled himself to the middle of nowhere.

"Never too fast when you find a sexy-as-all-get-out woman." Rafe wagged his eyebrows.

"You done, Dr. Phil?" Davis crossed his arms over his chest.

"For now."

"And don't talk about my sister like that. I can still beat you in hand-to-hand."

Rafe held his hands up in surrender and looked off to the side. "Speaking of the most beautiful woman in the world ..."

"Whatever." Piper took Rafe's seat he vacated for her.

Her arms held Davis's identical twin nephews. A

soft, pink blush colored Piper's cheeks as Rafe fussed to make sure she was comfortable. Even though Davis had worried about Piper when she first got together with Rafe, his sister beamed with happiness. She deserved someone who fawned over her like a lovesick puppy. That the man was Rafe, her secret crush she'd had forever, just made their love that much more special.

"Hey, Pipster." Davis smiled, his chest warming as he gazed upon the people he loved most in the world. "How are the munchkins?"

Piper launched into all the new things the boys had learned. Davis still couldn't believe Rafe had talked Piper into naming one of the boys Rex. The few times their teenage conversations had veered into that territory, Rafe had claimed he'd name his firstborn Rex, after the dinosaur. Davis didn't think he was actually serious, but Piper held Rex in her arms.

The kid was wild, living up to his name, even though he wasn't even one year old. He climbed all over his mom, pulling on her hair and grabbing for her nose. His brother, Dieter, lay calmly in Piper's other arm, sucking away on his thumb. His eyes followed his brother like he was either taking notes or just wanted his brother to chill for a moment.

Rex gripped Dieter's arm and yanked his hand away from his face. Dieter's face pinched into a scowl that had Davis snorting a laugh. Piper didn't miss a beat or a word in her story as she peeled Rex's fingers from Dieter's. Rex smiled and climbed up Piper's shoulder, while Dieter went back to sucking his thumb.

"I swear, it was like the two of them communicated their escape. One minute, they were both in the living room, playing. The next, they were climbing the kitchen shelves." Piper laughed, shaking her head. "Dieter literally let Rex climb onto his back so his brother could reach the higher shelf where the cookies are. I wish you could've been here to see it." Her smile faltered, then she pushed it back up. "Rafe caught it all on the security cameras. I'll have him email it over."

"Thanks. I'd like that." Davis hoped Piper didn't catch his fake cheerful tone.

What was he doing here, miles away from his family, bored out of his mind? He was missing so much of the boys' first year, and for what? Maybe Rafe was right, and Davis would get control of his issues better by talking to someone than by hiding.

He hated feeling bottled up when he was back in Colorado. He couldn't play bodyguard at Stryker Security Force anymore. It left him feeling like a shaken soda waiting to be opened. He wanted away from the violence and the need to watch his back all the time. Being there hadn't helped his constant sense of wariness. But what could he do if not that? He'd gotten into the military right out of high school.

All he knew was violence.

"How's the mining going? I bet it's beautiful up there." That's just like Piper, always wanting everyone to feel comfortable.

"It's okay. Been raining, so it makes life harder." Davis should do a better job at trying to make his sister not worry. "I like the peace out here, even with the rain. The other day, we had a sow and her two cubs wander into camp."

"No." Piper gasped and bounced the babies when they startled at her outburst.

"Yep."

"What did you do?"

"I was walking from my tent to the cabin for breakfast. I heard a whistle just as I cleared the bushes, and my head snapped up to the bears sniffing around the fire pit. Justin watched from his cabin door. They didn't even realize we were there until the mama started gnawing on the tires of the 4-wheeler, and Justin hollered at her to knock it off." Davis laughed, and it felt good. "Those bears took off so fast they looked like cartoon characters."

Piper smiled, her teary eyes hard to miss even through the screen. "It's so good to hear you laugh again."

He swallowed, hoping to dislodge the thickness in his throat. It didn't, so he whispered, "Yeah."

A loud fart blasted through the speakers, followed quickly by another. Piper lifted the babies away from her body, revealing two nasty spots on her shirt. Davis hadn't missed that part of being around his nephews.

"They poop in unison?" He chuckled as Piper gagged.

"Oh, gross." She gagged again. "Rafe!"

"Listen, it's been good talking." Davis couldn't hold in his laughter. "I'll call in a week or so if the weather cooperates."

"You better. Three weeks is too long." Piper glanced at the computer but snapped her attention back to Rex when he started climbing up her arm, leaving a trail. "Ew, sorry. I have to go."

"Love you, Pipster."

"Love you, too."

He clicked off just as she hollered louder for Rafe. An engine pulling up drew his attention from the image of his sister's disgusted face. He made it to the door of the cabin as Justin killed the engine with a punch. His face stormed and movements jerked. Looked like the conversation with the neighbors hadn't gone well.

An exploratory mining company had been on Justin for weeks, badgering him to sell out. His grandpa's will had passed the family claim down to Justin the year before. He had a lot of memories of summers spent here working the mine, and he'd told Davis there was no way he would sell now.

"So?" Davis leaned on the doorjamb.

"They've gone from a friendly offer to downright threats." Justin pushed past Davis and threw his hat on his bed.

"Do we need to contact the authorities?" Davis came up to the Alaskan wilderness to get away from trouble. Was it his lot in life to be filled with it?

"No. Not yet."

Justin paced the tiny open space in the twelve-by-twelve cabin, reminding Davis why he had set up the wall tent three-hundred feet away in a clearing in the bushes. This cabin was just too small for the both of them. Davis took a deep breath to calm the heating anger at his friend's news.

"I'm going back there tomorrow to tell them again that I'm not interested in any offer they have for me. They think I'm some podunk, back hills nobody." Justin huffed a humorless laugh. "If they knew all the things I've been through in the Special Forces, they'd know their threats won't do squat."

Justin was one of the best soldiers Davis knew. Serving with Justin had helped Davis see what loyalty and strength really were. It was why he agreed to come up here in the first place.

"Want me to come with you?" He'd go, though he couldn't guarantee he'd keep his cool like Justin would.

"Nah. No need. These big mining companies from China are used to people bending over for a stack of cash. There's nothing they can do if I refuse." Justin snatched his hat from the bed. "Might as well get some dirt moved while the weather is good."

Davis nodded and led the way to the mining area. It was probably better that he didn't go. The way his irritation tightened his shoulders, he'd end up doing something stupid and throw fuel on to the embers, flaring up the situation.

Chapter Three

Sunny tossed her pack into the back of her brother Tiikâan's Piper PA-18 and climbed in. Her brother adjusted her gear with a huff and strapped it down with a bungee cord. He'd been on her all morning to call the trip off, so if he was upset about her not stowing her gear correctly, she'd revel in her passive-aggressive action.

"You know I'm right." He shut the door and walked around the front of the plane, eyeing her the entire way. When he opened the pilot's door, he started right back in. "The weather's been horrible the last week. Instead of trekking through the normal muskeg and tundra, which is bad enough, you'll deal with swollen creeks and muddy terrain."

"So." Sunny fiddled with her camera, making sure it was ready to shoot.

"So? So, you get stuck in there, and I won't be able to come get you." He clicked on the engine, muttering under his breath about pain-in-the-butt little sisters.

She ignored her big, dumb brother's remarks. Kind of.

"Come on, Teeee-khaaan, when'd you turn into an old man?" She drew out his name and poked him in the arm.

He swatted her hand away. "I'm not an old man. I'm just smart. You don't know the Interior like I do."

"Really? If I remember right, I've climbed Denali more times than I have fingers to count. That doesn't include the other mountains I've summited around the world, you know … like that big one they call Everest. I've spent almost a month trekking across sea ice toward the North Pole, kayaked the Aleutian Islands on my own for a month, and spent my childhood hunting and camping in this area. And you're worried about me getting muddy?" She huffed a laugh and shook her head. "It's an adventure. It's supposed to be difficult."

"It's just—"

When he didn't continue, she turned in her seat. "It's just what?"

"I don't know. I have a bad feeling, is all." He pushed his hand through his hair. "Maybe it's just that I'm leaving for the North Slope tomorrow, and I won't be around if you need help."

Okay. Her big, dumb brother wasn't all that dumb, just a protective teddy bear. She leaned over and kissed his cheek. Too bad he had just gotten hired by a company up in Barrow to fly the company's executive around for the next few months. She might've been able to talk him into coming with her otherwise.

"Maybe you're more nervous about your own new adventure than you're letting on? I mean, it's kind of a deviation from your normal clientele." She poked him in the arm.

"Yeah. Catering to business execs is a heck of a lot different from hunters, but it will set me up for getting my guiding business to the next level."

"I'm excited for you, and when I get back from this trek, I might just fly up to Barrow to visit."

"Great. I'll put you to work as a copilot."

She tipped back her head and laughed. They both knew she'd never had much luck flying planes. Flipping her camera on, she pointed it at her brother.

"So, Captain Tiikâan, are we ready to fly?"

"Ready as we'll ever be. Buckle up, Sunshine." He winked at the camera and slid on his aviator glasses.

She could already see the comments rolling in from her female subscribers. They'd lost their minds over Gunnar's segments during the expedition to the North Pole. Seeing another good-looking Rebel man on the screen would be good for the ratings. She turned the camera to her, deciding to add fuel to the flames.

"He's single, ladies. Good with money, engines, and animals. He has a tender heart, a sturdy plane, and a smile to melt over."

"Sunniva May Rebel, you better not put that on your channel," he said as he fired up the propeller.

"What? I couldn't hear you over the noise."

"Oh, you heard me all right." He shook his head and lifted his hand at their parents standing off to the side of the short landing strip on their property.

Sunny turned the camera out the windshield and waved at her parents. She loved her family, but she couldn't leave soon enough. They all had questioned her going. She'd like to think she was strong enough that the requests hadn't tempted her to stay, but they had. Being alone had never been something she was good at. She blamed growing up in a big family. She'd rarely known what loneliness was.

Now … it consumed her.

But she needed it, right? Needed to grow up and do life on her own for a bit. She didn't want to be that person, always desperate for others. No, she wanted to be just as happy in her own company as when she had people around.

She filmed the Alaskan bush as they flew over tundra, rivers, and forests. When she got enough footage, she set the camera on her lap and gazed out the side window. She had a map and a compass, but seeing what she'd be trekking through left her slightly daunted.

Thirty minutes later, a gust of wind jerked the small plane just as the skies opened up and released a torrent. Tiikâan lifted an eyebrow at her in a told-you-so move. She just shrugged. A little rain never hurt anyone.

"We're two minutes from the sandbar," he said into her headphones.

Dragonflies zipped in her belly, making her more nauseous than the bucking plane. She gave a thumbs up and turned the camera back on.

"Okay, folks. The handsome pilot tells me we're getting close. Why don't you help me look for the sandbar we'll be landing on?" She pointed the lens out the windshield. "Up here, there aren't any landing strips, but thankfully, I've got the best bush pilot in Alaska. As long as there aren't any big obstacles on the sandbar, he'll be able to slide right down like Alaskan's own Nathan Blaine into home plate."

Tiikâan groaned. "He's a hockey player, Sunny, not baseball."

"Eh, whatever. He slides around, doesn't he?"

Her brother shook his head, not realizing she'd aimed the camera at him to see his reaction to her intentional mistake. "Yeah, but you can't be using the wrong sports terminology if you're going to throw it out there like that."

"He's Alaskan, a sports icon, and hot. Besides, you know I don't watch TV."

"Then how do you even know about him?" Tiikâan's exasperation built, and Sunny almost broke the joke by laughing.

"Well, he's Sawyer's dad and since Sawyer is about to be part of our family when Bjørn marries Sadie, I had to see what the buzz was about."

The Wilde family that Sunny's brother Bjørn was marrying into had lots of layers she was still learning. So far, she'd liked them all, but the fact that the famous hockey player was somehow connected had gotten her investigation skills going.

"That is so confusing, you know that, right?" Tiikâan glanced over at her.

Not able to hold her laughter in anymore, she bent over in a belly laugh that felt way too good. What a perfect way to start this trip.

"Real mature." Her brother rolled his eyes.

"Real gullible," she countered, and refocused on scanning for the sandbar.

They flew up the creek winding among the terrain like a river otter's trail through snow. Instead of the trail being clear, the water was the color of chocolate milk.

The clouds had dropped a ton of rain for it to look that way, especially how it foamed along the banks.

"It's fine. I wasn't crossing many creeks anyway," she whispered under her breath when trepidation threatened to make her turn home with her tail tucked between her legs.

"Ah … Houston, we have a problem." Tiikâan's voice in her headset startled her with a jerk.

"What?"

"The sandbar's flooded." He pointed out the window to the gentle curve in the creek.

Chocolate river rushed where the perfect landing spot used to be. She puffed her cheeks full with frustrated air. It was fine. They'd just go to Plan B.

"Let's head to that lake we marked on the GPS." She flipped the camera and smiled. "This is why it's good to have an alternate route in place, people! And it helps when your fantabulous pilot has floats."

"You sure?" Tiikâan peeked over at her.

"That you are fantabulous? Yeppers."

"No, that you still want to go?" Worry laced his response.

"Absolutely."

She couldn't afford to hesitate. If she did, she might never come back—might just take the carrot of a guiding job the climbing charter in Denali had offered her. She didn't want to walk the easy road anymore, taking opportunities that were comfortable. She wanted to blaze trails, which meant she couldn't let fear and solitude break her.

Chapter Four

DAVIS KICKED the generator hooked up to the trommel in frustration and wiped the rain from his face. If only Justin's grandpa had upgraded equipment at some point in this century. Maybe then they wouldn't spend so much time fixing, and more time actually mining. This heap of junk was probably older than Davis's aunt and uncle.

He stomped toward camp, his boots squishing with each step. He'd woken to the soft drizzle tapping on his canvas tent roof. Hoping for a few days break from the wet wasn't going to happen. Justin kept saying that the rain was abnormal. Supposedly, most summers in the Interior burned warm, if not hot, reaching into the eighties and nineties. Davis was beginning to think Justin was full of it.

As Davis passed the trail leading out of camp, he slowed and gazed down the dirt path. Justin should have been back. He'd left over an hour ago and hadn't planned to chitchat. Davis hurried the rest of the way to the cabin and wiped his feet on the plastic rug on the stoop. If Justin didn't return in fifteen, Davis would head over to see what the holdup was.

All morning, anxiety had crawled like ants along his body. He couldn't explain it, but he'd learned in the military not to ignore the feeling. Before Justin left, Davis had asked again if he should go. Now he wished he would have insisted.

He searched the room for the toolbox, his tension morphing to aggravation when he couldn't find it. "Can't anything here be where it's supposed to be?"

The tap of the drizzle on the metal roofing was his only answer. Growling low, he marched back out the door. When he kicked an empty milk crate across the yard to release his anger, his foot slipped on the slick ground, sending him sprawling. Cold mud soaked through his pants and covered his face.

He wanted to roar at the world pitted against him, but it wouldn't do any good. He could either continue to throw a tantrum like a toddler, or he could pull himself together and get back to work. Blowing out a deep breath, he pushed his hands into the squishy mud and got to his knees.

"Okay. You win." He sat back on his heels and lifted his head to the rain.

It's refreshing cold splashed upon his eyelids and tracked through the beard he'd let grow since arriving. He huffed out the last of his frustration. Maybe Justin was taking so long because he was working things out. Davis didn't always have to jump to the worst-case scenario. Just because he saw potential treachery around every corner didn't mean there actually was.

He eased up to his feet. His muscles weighed a thousand pounds as he trudged to his tent to change. All this worry couldn't be good for him. He hardly slept, got heartburn every time he ate, and headaches pounded almost every day. Maybe he should talk to someone about what had happened. Justin had been in the military and would understand.

Could Davis open up, though?

Confess how his gullibility killed honorable men and left him to live with the guilt?

He swallowed down the burn of regret and pushed the flap to his wall tent open. Heat from the fire he'd lit that morning in the tiny barrel stove warmed his chilled skin. While the living area was small, it worked. He had enough space for a cot with a large tote pushed against the foot for his gear, a one-person table he'd thrown together with scrap wood, a chair, and about four feet of walking room.

He stripped off his coat and draped it over the back of his chair. The toolbox he'd thrown a fit over sat on the table with the four wheeler carburetor he'd been working on the day before. He puffed a laugh and yanked off his wet shirt. Talking needed to be top of his list, because he was obviously losing his mind.

Chapter Five

Sunny adjusted the two ropes looped over her shoulders and crossing her chest bandolier-style and checked the camera to make sure it still filmed. It had a protective cover, and the battery had a full charge when she got moving two hours earlier. Still, the constant drizzle worried her.

"All right, folks. Today hasn't been much better than yesterday or last night. That's the thing about adventures. You never know what weather you're gonna get. Alaska isn't a tame walk in the park, either." She smiled, then connected it back to the mount strapped across her chest.

She hadn't talked much during that morning, which wasn't like her. Usually, the continual one-sided conversation she had with her viewers kept the loneliness from sinking in. This trip, the trick didn't work. She just felt empty, lacking.

Hopefully, the rain kept her spirits down and not the desire to be done with the whole solo adventuring gig.

She didn't even want to think about how many times the temptation to use the InReach satellite communication clipped to her belt loop to get a flight out had burned. Only the embarrassment of quitting kept her from texting her parents. She wasn't slated to contact them until that night, so she had to get the forlornness off her shoulders before then, or she might not be able to keep her fingers from typing the evac code.

She reached the top of a knoll and scanned the stretch of terrain before her. Forest and hills filled this area, with the occasional meadow opening the space up. One such flat space filled the base of the knoll. From up there it looked flat and inviting, but the cusps of willows could grow thick, and miles of muskeg could mask as meadow and make the trek torturous. She generally took the bright side of situations, so she was banking on good, solid ground that provided an easy and steady hike for a while.

A thin, gray trail of smoke twirled into the sky in the distance along the willows. She pulled out her binoculars and surveyed the camp. An excavator parked in a muddy pit next to an old John Deere dozer that had probably been built the same year her grandpa was born. A trommel was positioned next to a couple of tarps stretched over a table like a canopy. She didn't see anyone roaming around, but the smoke definitely meant someone was there.

She lowered her binoculars and bit the side of her bottom lip. She might be on a solo trek, but there wasn't anything saying that she couldn't stop in and visit. Wasn't that an important part of survival—using what, or in this case, who you found to get you to your destination? Growing up, she'd been to every Fortymile Miners Association picnic each year with her parents. Every person she'd met had been friendly enough, though some could be a tad salty.

The need to talk with someone—anyone—pulled at her so strongly her feet moved toward the camp without conscious thought. She'd just let whoever was down there know she wouldn't post any information or videos of their actual mining operation. Miners were notoriously protective of their claims.

"We are in luck, people. An important part of survival is using all the resources you find, and we just found a big one." She jogged down the knoll, suddenly full of energy. "When you are in the wilderness, finding other people, even abandoned homesteads, could be the difference between life and death. Now, I'm not in a precarious situation, but I might get a meal before heading on. Later down the trail, that meal today could mean that my supplies last me another day."

At the prospect of seeing people, her chattiness was back. She smiled at herself as she slowed to a walk. Though she stretched her steps wide, she didn't want to startle the miners by rushing in. Getting shot would prematurely end her long-term plans, whatever those ended up being.

She slowed as she came to the open mine area. There still wasn't anyone about, so she skirted the excavator and headed toward the skinny trail disappearing into the willows on the opposite side of the space. As she passed the trommel, she froze. Freedom Mining was painted in bright red, white, and blue across the metal side. She squealed, doing a little dance that splashed mud up her boots.

"Folks, I can't believe it, but this claim is our friend Justin's place." She rushed to the trail. "He served in the military with my siblings. I don't even know how many times he's been to my parents' for picnics and whatnot. I may just camp here for the night. Catching up with friends is too good of an opportunity to pass. I'm going to shut up now and try to surprise him. I can't wait to see the shocked look on his face when he sees me just walk out of the woods."

She squeezed her mouth closed. Excitement bubbled up in her, and she didn't trust herself not to keep from chattering away. This day just went from a total downer to the best day in weeks.

She hadn't even considered she'd run into Justin's claim, not with thousands of square miles of wilderness in the Interior. Most people don't realize just how massive the land is. That was one thing that frustrated Tiikâan about guiding hunters. The hunters got upset with her brother when there weren't any animals to hunt. Sure, Alaska had more moose, caribou, and bears than any other state, but it was also larger than Texas, California, and Montana combined.

The sound of tires splashing through puddles hit her just as she spied Justin through the branches. She rushed down the last few feet of the path. Her smile stretched her cheeks so they hurt. He was going to flip out. Justin didn't see her as she stepped from the path into the opening, his attention glued on two men rounding the front of a side-by-side.

As one man lifted a pistol, she skidded to a halt, her body freezing colder than sea ice. Three shots blasted rapidly from the gun, jerking Justin as they hit. Her pulse roared in her ears. She vaguely registered her scream as Justin fell to the ground. Bright red mixed with the chocolate brown of the puddle he landed in.

"Hey!" A shout yanked her attention to the men as the shooter turned the gun on her.

Chapter Six

DAVIS BUTTONED his flannel shirt as tires driving up filtered back to his tent. Amazing how loud a sound like that could crash through the melody of the wilderness. It reminded him of missions in the quiet desert when they'd wait for hours for a single vehicle to drive by. The break in the silence had always made his hair stand on end, kind of like it did now.

He reached his hand toward the wood stove for a few more seconds of warmth before he went to see how the confrontation went. Three shots exploded, and Davis tore out of his tent toward the cabin. Justin sprawled on his back in the mud, his face turned away from Davis. An unfamiliar side-by-side parked behind Justin's four-wheeler, but no one was around.

Davis slid on his knees to Justin's side, carefully covering his hands over the blood flowing from the bullet holes in Justin's chest. Too much blood. How could they get an evacuation here in time?

"Hold on, buddy." Davis reached for the front of

Justin's shirt to tear it open and assess what could be done, but Justin's hand stopped him.

"Go … help … girl." What was Justin talking about?

There weren't any girls around here.

"Shh, let me work."

"No, Davis. Too late for me." Justin looked down the trail, then back at Davis, his fingers tightening around Davis's, his eyes hard with determination. "Hiker in the woods. Shooters chased. Go help her."

"But—" Tears of agony and rage tightened Davis's throat and blurred his vision.

How could he possibly leave Justin?

"Fields, I'm not going to make it." Justin squeezed Davis's hand again, then sagged into the ground like all his energy had leeched out with his blood. "But you can … save her."

The last words whispered up to Davis. He knew, like Justin, that the wounds were fatal, especially up there in the middle of nowhere. Davis clenched his fist, his entire body shaking with impotency.

"I love you, brother," he choked out.

Justin nodded, a tear tracking down his cheek. "Love you, too. Now … go."

Davis ground his teeth together so hard he thought they'd crack, then bolted toward the trail. Adrenaline coursed through him as he let the rage free. Whoever did this to Justin would pay.

The mud made the tracks easy to follow. One set of smaller footprints led two others away from camp. So, there were two men, not just one.

The small prints veered into the willows. *Smart.* With the density of the small trees, it'd be harder to pursue.

Hopefully, whoever she was could move faster through the tight forest than the shooters.

Davis dove into the woods, ignoring how the limbs grabbed and tore at his sleeves. If he'd been thinking, he would've grabbed the rifle from the cabin. He had nothing, not even a coat, but the military had trained him for this in the special ops division of the army called the Delta Force.

He didn't need a weapon to take down these guys.

He just needed surprise.

A shout sounded ahead and focused his direction. The *ta-ta-ta* of a semi-automatic firing pushed his legs even faster. He'd have to get to the girl first and find her a safe hiding spot. Then he could circle back and take care of the two men who killed his friend. Because there was no way he'd let them go without retribution.

Chapter Seven

Sunny barreled through the willows, ducking as bullets whizzed by. Rain and branches pelted her face, obstructing her vision. It could also be the tears rushing down her face. She couldn't stop them, not with terror building in her brain like a microburst in a thunderstorm. Any minute and it'd let loose, shattering what little thought process she had left.

Her pack snagged on a tree and yanked her backwards. She lurched forward and ripped it free. Maybe she should drop her pack? She went to unbuckle it as another round of bullets zipped by. One pinged against her gear with a deafening crunch, and she jerked her hand away from the buckle.

It wasn't much, but the pack offered some protection. She hefted it up and veered into a tighter bunch of willows. Besides, if she dropped her pack, she'd have nothing—no shelter, no food, no communication—nothing. Best to keep the thing on.

She needed to find better ground that didn't tell the

men exactly where she was going. Where was a good muskeg swamp or muddy creek when she needed it?

"She's near. Split up." A man's yell came way too close.

How would she get away from them? She was going to die out there in the wilderness all alone, and no one would find her body or know what happened. Her parents would freak, search the entire wilderness for her, but the bears or wolves would probably get to her carcass first.

Why? Why did she ever think solo trekking through Alaska's rough terrain was a smart idea?

To be fair, she'd expected to run into bears or moose, not homicidal psychopaths. She shook her head to clear it of the vision of Justin's shocked expression. The men hadn't even said anything, just started firing.

Oh, Lord, Justin.

Sunny growled and shook her head again to clear her tears. She couldn't think about that. Couldn't let her grief distract her. Dark spots swam in her vision, and she took as deep a breath as she could.

The temptation to look back clawed at her. She pushed it down. If she didn't focus on what was ahead of her, she'd trip, and they'd be on her like a pack of starving wolves.

A shadow darted through the willows beside her. She clamped her mouth closed against the scream that wanted loose. There was no way she'd give them the satisfaction of hearing her cry out again. Besides, if they'd split up, she might be able to overpower one.

But only if she didn't give her position away to the other.

She willed her legs to move faster. The shadow disappeared. Had she just seen things in her fear?

Focusing back on the trees before her, she gasped when they disappeared to a small clearing.

"This way, quick," a low voice said right next to her.

A hand clamped around her bicep, sending freezing terror through her. She exploded, not thinking of what to do, just reacting. She threw her elbow up, connecting with a crack to her attacker's nose. Spinning low, she knocked her opponent's legs out from under him. The weight of her pack unbalanced her and sent her to the ground as well. She scrambled away, trying to gain her feet in the slippery moss and mud.

"Ma'am. I'm here to hel—" The man grunted as she kicked his hands away.

Did he really think she'd listen?

She got to her feet, but he grabbed her legs, face planting her into the mud. He spoke again, but she couldn't hear his words over the roaring in her ears. He rolled her over, and she erupted into a flurry of punches and kicks. She wasn't thinking, just doing everything she could to get away and keep alive. His hands kept snatching at hers, making it impossible to get a hold of any weapon to help her.

She didn't want to die there.

Didn't want to draw her last breath alone.

Mud smeared down her face into her eyes. She couldn't make out her attacker. He was simply a shadowy form. Probably for the best. If she was going to die, she really didn't want to watch him pull the trigger.

"I'm trying to help. Please, stop," the man demanded again in a low, harsh whisper.

No way. She'd never stop. She'd fight like a rabid

wolverine to her death. At least then, she'd go down with the pride and courage worthy of her family's heritage.

A blow hit her head like a sledgehammer.

Forceful.

Blunt.

She tasted metal. Her ears rang and vision tunneled. Then, sound and sight disappeared. The silence was deafening … terrifying.

Chapter Eight

Sharp pain radiated up his elbow where it had accidentally connected with the woman's head. He cursed low when all her muscles relaxed but was thankful the little wildcat wasn't fighting him anymore. Now to just get her away from the men so he could explain that he wasn't the enemy without dodging feet and fists.

"Shoot," he whispered as he climbed over her pack and rolled her over. "I didn't mean to—Sunny?" He wiped his fingers across her bronzed, muddied cheek. "No. No, no, no."

His blood froze in his veins as he stared at the woman he'd secretly daydreamed about showing up since he'd arrived. Only he didn't want her there like this, in this moment, with killers' footsteps snapping branches not a hundred yards away. He had to get her somewhere safe.

Carefully, he unclipped her pack and slung it over his back. He pushed the almost black hair plastered to her forehead out of her eyes, then lifted her into his arms. The last time he'd seen Sunny, they'd both been in Kentucky, watching her sister Lena's stepson, Carter, while Lena and Marshall went on their honeymoon. Sunny had volunteered to nanny, and Lena had assigned Davis as extra protection.

They'd only spent three weeks together in Kentucky, but it had been the first time in years that he'd felt like there might be a future for him beyond the darkness he'd lived in. Sunny had had such hope on her face when he'd dropped a comment about maybe spending the summer up in Alaska.

When she woke and the reality of who he was crashed in, he doubted he'd see anything in her dark, brown eyes but hate and pain. With the way he'd gone silent after she'd left, he'd deserve it.

Threading his way through the willows, he stopped now and then to listen for her pursuers. He pushed down the worry that she wasn't waking. He'd witnessed men sometimes take hours to rouse after being knocked out. It didn't happen often and usually ended with the dude being razzed for it. He just prayed Sunny didn't come up fighting and yelling, thinking she was still in the midst of the struggle.

He gritted his teeth, hating that he'd added to her fear. He'd tried to tell her he was there to help her. There hadn't been a better way to get her attention without making more noise. He'd had to stay quiet to keep the men from knowing he was there.

Didn't matter now. The men's shouting in the distance signaled they'd lost the trail. Davis had bought some time when he'd accidentally whacked Sunny in the head.

He adjusted his hold on her, lifting her tighter

against him. She sure gave him a fight. He wouldn't expect anything less from a Rebel, but how she'd kept her head and not called out impressed the heck out of him. Most people would have screamed.

He came to the base of a hill. The willows thinned out to birch trees. As he skirted the bottom, he scanned the hillside for somewhere to hide. The shouts shifted their direction. He had no more time. Without the cover of the willows, they'd be found, and he didn't have a weapon to protect them with.

His eyes snagged on a darker shadow about two-thirds of the way up the hill. He backed up, careful to keep his steps on the fallen leaves and moss rather than the mud, and ducked down. It looked like the hill had sloughed off around a cusp of birch, creating an alcove. Hopefully, there wasn't a bear or wolverine or something already occupying the space. That was the last thing he needed now.

Only one way to find out. He hefted Sunny over his shoulder in a fireman's hold. He hated to do it and hoped she didn't wake up, but he couldn't make it up the hill cradling her. Picking his way carefully to leave as little trace of where they'd gone as possible, he hiked the hill. His chest heaved when he made it to the spot he'd spied. If it wouldn't work to hide in, he'd tuck them up on the hill and hope for the best.

He gently laid Sunny on the moss outside the alcove and ducked inside, slipping his small Maglite out of his pocket. He traced the rough walls with the light, surprised at the size of the indention. When no animal jumped out and clawed his face, he set the light against the side of the cave and went back to Sunny.

The crack of a twig and the angry chatter of a

squirrel snapped Davis's gaze to the bottom of the hill. The men stomped along the path Davis had just taken. How had the men found his trail so quickly? He'd been so careful with his steps.

Cold sweat traced down his spine. He shivered. These men were better trained than he first thought. They had the look of some of the shadier private contractors he'd run into overseas. Why would an exploratory mine need mercenaries?

He grabbed Sunny by the arm and dragged her into the alcove without taking his eyes off the men. If they spotted Sunny or Davis, he'd have to take off up the hill and pray for divine intervention. He didn't deserve it, but Sunny surely did.

When he safely tucked her behind him, he set a few branches over the drag marks in the moss and watched the men through the exposed roots of the trees. One man's head jerked ahead of him, and he pointed. Davis's gaze swung to where the man indicated, and Davis stifled a groan. On the leaves, where he'd hoisted Sunny up, bunched a bright pink swatch of fabric.

The men rushed on it like wolves on an injured caribou calf. The one who'd spotted it lifted it and sniffed the handkerchief, elbowing his friend with a smile as he handed the fabric to him. Davis couldn't make out their words as the other man took a hit like a druggie who'd been without for a long time. Davis clenched his fingers around a root. Sunny always smelled like lemons and sunshine, making him want to linger. From the men's lecherous smiles, they now had other ideas besides just murder in their minds.

Each man scanned the ground, searching for footsteps. One surveyed the hillside, and Davis held his breath. If they came up here, there was nowhere for him and Sunny to go. With her still unconscious, and Davis having to carry her, the men would be on them before he could get them to the top of the hill.

That was if they didn't just open fire from where they stood.

Why hadn't Davis grabbed the rifle or any weapon? All he had on him were a tiny flashlight and his pocketknife. The Leatherman had a lot of tools, but none of them would help him against two men with guns.

The man took a step toward the hill and leaned forward. Even from up there, Davis could see the man squinting. Davis let out a breath and released his tension like the Special Forces had taught him.

Hopefully, they hadn't noticed the difference in footprint size or seen the scuffed-up spot where he and Sunny had fought. If they still thought she was alone, he had the element of surprise going for him. He could overpower one of them and use their weapon against the remaining man. Whatever happened next, he'd fight to his last breath before he let these men get Sunny.

Chapter Nine

Sunny sucked in a breath of loamy air, her arms and legs numb and heavy. She needed to move. This guy was on her, would kill her any second.

Blinking to clear the pain pounding in her head, she punched at the dark shadow coming to her. Why was it so dark? He grabbed her hands, and she jerked away.

"Sunny, it's me, Davis," the shadow whispered so low she almost couldn't hear it over the loud ringing in her ears, but that made little sense.

She shook her head.

It was a ploy.

He was trying to trick her.

As he reached for something off to the side, she bunched to explode. She wouldn't go down, dazed like an idiot. He moved his hand up to his face, shining the small flashlight on him. Davis Fields's handsome face had a dark, scruffy beard hiding his dimples. His hair had grown longer since last fall, but his dark, storm-gray eyes pierced her the same. Every muscle relaxed on a whooshed sob.

"Davis?"

How was he here?

This had to be a dream. She reached out to him to see if he was real. The touch of his fingers on hers shattered the last of her fight, and she launched herself into his arms.

He was here.

She wasn't alone.

She was safe.

"Shh, Firefly. We're not out of danger yet." His calm whisper of his nickname for her against her ear brought all her walls back up.

He might be here with her now, but he hadn't called like he said he would. Hadn't responded to her texts after she'd left Kentucky. He'd well and truly ghosted her, so throwing herself at the man just proved her pathetic nature.

Granted, she'd just witnessed her friend's murder, been chased by men bent on killing her, and fought harder than she'd ever fought before in her life. So, hugging the man who had probably just saved her was simply gratitude.

Lingering in the hug?

Pure, selfish desire.

Which she needed to squash.

She pushed away from him. "What's going on? Where are we?"

When his hands smoothed up her back, her insides warmed like a Care Bear, from the old VHS tapes her mom had let them watch growing up, when they did that belly shine thing. *Nope.* She couldn't let those buzzing, warm feelings happen, not with Davis.

Not again.

She sat back and pulled her knees into her chest. The flash of hurt on Davis's face was quick, but she still caught it. Too bad if her pulling away hurt him. She dashed her fingers over her cheeks, wiping away the last of the tears. If they weren't safe, she had to stay alert.

He tipped his head to the side and turned to peer out a bunch of roots crisscrossing over the opening. She did a quick assessment of their surroundings, wondering how he found this tight alcove, and crawled up beside him. At the base of the hill, the two men who had killed Justin and chased her talked while they walked back and forth along the decayed leaves left from last fall. The shooter twirled her handkerchief around his finger as he paced.

She touched her neck. How had the thing even fallen off? She glared at Davis's profile. How had he subdued her? She cringed at the headache pounding on her left temple and turned back to the men below. She'd get answers from Davis later. What mattered at that moment was if the men found their trail.

The shooter glanced up, and she held her breath. What would they do if the men climbed the hill? She hated not knowing what the terrain and their situation was.

The other man shouted, tearing the shooter's gaze from finding their hiding spot. They both studied the leaves, the shooter's friend pointing at what he thought was a trail. The shooter nodded and tipped his head the way his friend pointed. After scanning the hillside, then his back trail, the shooter followed his friend into the willows.

Sunny exhaled and scampered away from the roots until her back pressed to the dirt wall of the overhang.

They had bought some time. Should they move now or wait? She ran her shaking hands through her hair, cringing when dirt sprinkled her face.

"What the heck are you doing here, Sunny?" Davis turned a quarter of a turn, his face creased in anger.

"I … I'm hiking."

"Did you know Justin was here? Had you planned on visiting him?" The way he peppered the questions, and the tone laced behind the upset, made her feel guilty.

She ruffled at that thought. She had done nothing wrong. Hadn't planned a rendezvous with Justin or anything, if that's what Davis was implying. Was he jealous? Was that why he was mad?

"I didn't know *anyone* was here, let alone Justin. Or you, for that matter." *You big jerk.* She kept that last bit to herself. "I saw the mine while I was scouting and stopped in for a visit."

"Because dropping in unannounced at a gold mine is a perfectly okay thing to do." Davis shook his head and glanced out the roots.

Sunny glared at him. All Care Bear-glowing, warm and fuzzy feelings vanished.

"We need to get you out of here." Davis talked to the roots like they'd help him evacuate her.

"You mean *us*. We need to get us out of here."

When he shook his head, her frustration with him leeched to cold fear.

"What are you going to do, go Rambo and hunt these guys down?"

"Exactly."

"No. *No*, not on your own, you aren't." She grabbed his shoulder and yanked him around. "Listen, we use my InReach and alert the authorities. Both Gunnar and Bjørn will be here in a matter of hours, plus whatever troopers would come."

"We can call. Find a spot farther away from here where you can be picked up, and I'll leave a trail for whoever comes to follow." He crossed his arms over his chest. "But I'm not letting Justin's murderers disappear."

Sunny rolled her eyes and reached for her emergency beacon. She wasn't about to argue with him, not at the moment, at least. There was no way she'd let him go on his own. If he wouldn't let her stay with him, she'd just follow. It wasn't like he'd tie her to a tree or something.

She unclipped the InReach handheld from her pack and turned it on. Nothing but silence, and no signal greeted her.

Goosebumps covered her already chilled skin. That can't be right. This gadget worked at the North Pole. Why wouldn't it be working? How would they get help now?

Davis took the gadget from her hands and fiddled with the buttons. When it was clear the thing wouldn't work, he cursed and chucked a rock against the opposite wall. Dirt flew from the impact, and she jerked.

Pulling her knees closer, she ground her teeth together to keep them from chattering. She understood his frustration. Shoot. She wanted to throw stuff around too.

"What are we going to do now?" She shivered, the dampness finally seeping in with her adrenaline zapped.

Davis gazed at her across the small space and, with a sigh, moved beside her. "I need to get back to camp. There's a computer in Justin's cabin we can call out on."

"Okay."

She leaned into his side when he put his arm across her shoulder. It wasn't because she was glad to see him. More like his heat eased a bit of her tension.

Oh, who was she kidding?

All kinds of emotions flooded her at once—relief, hope, even happiness. She just needed to remember that she couldn't trust those emotions.

That she couldn't trust him.

With her safety, yes. He was one of the country's most elite soldiers. She just couldn't depend on him when it came to her heart.

Chapter Ten

Nine Months Earlier

Day 31: Fake Relationship with a Real-Life Hero

Sunny came in from running the dogs the ten-mile trail with the four-wheeler. The long ride through the crisp autumn Alaskan air had helped her clear her head from the doubts and pain swirling there. If she wanted to stay sane, she couldn't hope for a different reality like she was, especially not when the solitude of wintering in Chicken set in.

Marching to her old room in her parents' place, she snatched her phone from the charger and turned it on. As the screen came alive, she promised herself this would be the last time that she checked her phone for a text from Davis. Her heart couldn't take the hope that built only to crash when nothing was there.

She tapped on her messages, then opened the short text conversation they'd had. Nothing more from him besides his initial "Glad you made it home safe" text over a week and a half ago. Her heart crashed to the floor and eyes blurred. Heaving a sigh, she slumped onto her bed.

Obviously, she'd read more into their friendship than he had. The thought that it was all fake twisted her gut. She really was a bad judge of character.

She closed her eyes and shook her head against the memories that had taunted her all week.

Memories of the way Davis had looked at her.

Held her.

Kissed her.

They'd had so much fun together watching Carter that it hadn't felt like it was pretend. The image of his expression the night they'd camped out in the backyard came to mind. It was like he'd had to rip those words of him leaving Stryker from his soul. As he'd opened that jar of fireflies, he'd looked so serious—so lost—she'd wanted to wrap him in her arms and tell him it'd be okay.

Well, the joke was on her.

He'd probably been faking that, too. Wasn't that what a pretend relationship was all about? Real life wasn't like in the movies or romance novels where the fake becomes true. If she didn't always look at the positive side of people and situations, she'd know that.

It was good she was spending the winter with only her dogs and taciturn brother to keep her company. In fact, taking life solo for a while sounded like a smart plan.

No more guiding.

No more men.

Just her and whatever adventure nature threw at her. At least then, the only thing that could possibly get hurt was her body, not her heart. With a nod of determination, she went back to her text list, swiped Davis's name and picture left, and hit the red trash icon.

———

Davis pulled Sunny closer as she shivered beneath his arm. He had to move, find a place safe for Sunny to wait, then circle back to the mine. He could make a call to Fort Wainwright in Fairbanks and have troops there in less than two hours. Then, he'd take them to the exploratory mining operation and find out what in this Alaskan wilderness caused the company to murder over. While he waited for reinforcements, he'd do some hunting of his own. He had two men that needed to get lost permanently to the wilds.

He squeezed his eyes tight and leaned his head back against the dirt wall. Sunny couldn't see his struggle to keep the lid on his anger. She didn't deserve the overflow. That display of rage with the rock was more than enough.

Wasn't that why he'd come up to this God-forsaken area?

Because no matter how hard he tried to keep a handle on his emotions, those closest to him got hurt. He'd seen how his well-placed barbs could crumble his sister's demeanor. Back at the Stryker complex, the more he picked at or grumped, the more the guys had stopped pulling their punches during training. He'd welcome it, thinking he'd needed the release the pain of a fist brought.

Now, he realized it had just been a temporary fix, like a piece of duct tape on a rusted radiator. Any minute and the tape would come loose and steam would shoot out. He needed true healing, a real handle on his reactions and emotions. Alaskan mining with Justin had been that place of moving on for him.

"We have to go," Davis said gruffly, pushing away from Sunny as the thoughts of Justin's death assaulted him and made Davis shake.

"Okay."

She rubbed her hands together before tucking them under her armpits. Her chin quivered a second before she stifled it. He needed to get her warm. It might be summer, but hypothermia could still set in, especially with the drizzle not letting up.

"What's the plan?" She shifted and reached for her pack.

He pushed her hand away and wrapped his hand around the straps. "First, we move up the hill. Try to keep your steps on the moss and leaves. We want to hide our tracks as much as we can. It'll be hard with how wet it is."

"Channel my Athabaskan stealth-hunting heritage. Got it."

His lips twitched on one side. She had told him when they'd been in Kentucky that she wished she'd had more time with her mother's grandma. Sunny had loved the stories of her ancestors and said she spent so much time outside because of how it made her feel closer to her great-grandma.

"Once we get some distance away from here, we'll find a place for you to hole up while I circle back to the mine." Davis crawled toward the entrance.

"Wait. What?" Sunny snagged his arm and pulled him back. "I'm not hiding."

"It's not safe."

"Duh, Captain Commando." She rolled her eyes. "That's why you need me."

His head shook before she even finished her sentence. "I've done this a thousand times. Special Forces, remember?"

"With back up, or do you not remember them?" Her voice snapped with sarcasm.

Man, even angry, she shined. He couldn't risk her getting hurt or caught. Couldn't trust himself with her safety, not with how his PTSD could make him snap in rage or freeze solid with fear.

"Sunny, I've been trained for exactly this. Spent years in the army doing nothing but sneaking around."

"And what do you think all those years I've been bow hunting have been?" She pushed his shoulder. "Do you know how hard it is creeping within twenty feet of a thousand-pound bull moose and not be detected? Or what about a dall sheep on the open rocky mountainside or a full-grown grizzly? Darn near impossible, which is why most hunt with rifles."

"Sunny—"

"No, don't Sunny me." She gripped his sleeve in her fingers. "You're not leaving me, Davis."

Her fingers trembled against his arm. If anything happened to her, he'd hate himself for agreeing to let her come.

He cupped her cheek in his hand. "Okay, Firefly. You win."

Her smile almost blinded him, so he pulled his hand away and quickly continued in his sternest tone.

"You follow everything that I say. *Everything*." He cocked his eyebrow at her.

"Yes, sir." She saluted.

"I'm serious, Sunny. If I tell you to run, you run. No questions, and I promise I'll be right behind you."

"Follow orders. Got it." She reached for her pack. "You might not believe this, but my dad ran a tight ship. Sure, I'm used to being the leader, but I know when to give the helm to someone more qualified."

"I know. I'm just … scared." There. He said it.

"Me too." Her serious gaze stared at him over a trembling smile. "We've got this."

She reached toward her pack, and he shook his head when she pulled her bag to her. "I'll carry it until we get close to camp. Save your strength."

"Fine. Let's go." She peered through the roots toward where the men disappeared. "No baddies this way."

He eased out of the shelter and scanned the area for shadows that didn't belong. When he saw none, he hoisted her pack over his shoulders and motioned her up the hill. When she made it halfway to the top, he followed.

As he crested the rise, he found her searching the area like a true soldier. All her bubbly personality had dissipated to intense focus. Maybe they *could* do this together.

He nodded at her, hiked her pack higher on his shoulders, and circled back toward the mine. No one could call her weak. Her pack weighed a ton. It reminded him of all those missions he'd had to haul gear for days on end.

As they walked within a quarter mile of Justin's mine, a dark plume of smoke rose from the trees.

"Davis." Sunny spoke his name low, almost inaudibly.

"I see it." He looked back at her, not wanting her to go any closer. If whoever had caught the cabin on fire was still there, she'd be in even more danger.

"Don't even think about it." She pushed past him and disappeared into the willows.

He huffed a laugh and let his smile free. There really wasn't anything worth grinning about. Yet, his Firefly still knew how to light up his darkness, even after he blew it with her the first time.

Chapter Eleven

Sunny slinked through the willows, though in her mind she stomped. Stupid Davis and his dumb, handsome looks of concern. *Ugh.* He'd met her family. Shoot, the big lug fought alongside three of her siblings. Did he honestly think she was so far removed from her brothers and sister that she couldn't handle this?

Sure, having him close and the way his gaze lingered on her face like she mattered to him made her gut pop like kernels in Grandma's hand-crank popcorn maker. If Sunny wasn't careful, those kernels would burn and become an acrid, stinking mess. The kind that takes forever to get out.

Kind of like the smoke that got stronger the closer they weaved their way through the forest.

She needed to remember how he'd just disappeared on her last fall. His expressions he thought he hid screamed he'd do it again. There was no way she could trust that he wouldn't leave her behind.

Her solo adventuring flew out the window the instant those shots shattered her world. She'd cling to

Davis like industrial-strength Velcro if she had to. Yes, because she needed him, but he needed her too. Even if all she did was keep him from doing something royally shortsighted, like going in all rogue G.I. Joe, thinking he could take down these people single-handedly.

Davis's hand touched her shoulder, and she jerked, her heart jumping into her throat. She peeked back at him, lifting her eyebrow and praying he couldn't see her pulse pounding in her neck. He touched his ear and tipped his head to the north. She held her breath and focused her eyes in that direction. A vehicle approached. How he'd heard that faint sound in the distance amazed her. He might actually have her beat with his super soldier skills.

He made some hand movements that she interpreted he wanted her to follow as they moved forward. She nodded. He'd already made her promise she'd follow his lead. Might as well let him go in first.

As he rushed through the willows, she marveled at his ability to move quickly without a sound or brush on the trees to give away their location. Even with her heavy pack strapped to him, he made it look effortless.

The roar of a fire and snap of wood and glass burning filled the air, and approaching quietly wasn't as dire as before. Davis stopped behind a thick blueberry bush threaded with fireweed blooming high over it. The purple flowers hid them, making it easier to peer through the green shrubs at the homestead.

Flames already licked up the log walls of the small cabin and danced out the door. Were they not worried about a forest fire? If the computer Davis planned on using had been in there, it was toast. Her shoulders slumped. How would they get help now?

A jeep pulled up behind the side-by-side from earlier and a 4-wheeler that hadn't been there before. An Asian man who held himself with command meandered up to another man who walked out from behind the cabin carrying a gas can.

"Is our problem handled?" The bored tone of the boss man's voice carried over flames and chilled Sunny to the bone.

"Mr. Freedom's had an unfortunate accident." The other man peered toward the cabin, tossing the can toward the cabin. "It appears he died tragically in a house fire."

"Pity." Boss Man's smirk held no remorse.

Davis lurched forward.

Sunny wrapped her arms around him. "No."

"But he—" Davis growled, his entire body shaking with rage.

"I know." She choked on a sob and leaned her forehead to his. "I know."

"They need to pay." His muscles bunched like he would pounce.

"Don't leave me, Davis." She cupped his face with both hands, praying with all her might that he wouldn't barge out there and get himself killed. "Please, I need you."

He fisted his hands into her rain jacket and sucked in long, deep breaths. She stayed with her head to his, mimicking each of his inhales and exhales. When a tear leaked from his eye, she wiped it with her thumb.

He spread his hands wide across her back, pulling her into his powerful arms and burying his face in her neck. He took one last breath, then released her just as quickly.

"We need to leave." He grabbed her hand, adjusting his position to backtrack.

"And just where have you two been?" the fire starter hollered, freezing Sunny where she crouched.

"We have a slight problem," Justin's murderer said as he came into view.

"Well?" Irritation laced Boss Man's voice.

"A woman witnessed the murder," the other guy that had chased her responded.

"Woman?" Fire Starter asked.

"A backpacker. Came out of the woods just as we took care of business." The murderer motioned toward the trail Sunny had come down earlier.

"Did you get rid of her?" The menace in Boss Man's voice skated down her back like sharp fingernails.

The murderer shifted on his feet, and his partner glared at him before answering. "No. She got away."

Boss Man shook his head in disappointment, and both men fidgeted in unease. "Find her. Whatever it takes. If you don't, only the wolves will know where your carcasses lie."

Davis pulled on Sunny's arm, yanking her away from the bushes.

"Follow close," he whispered in her ear. "Quietly."

She swallowed the fear building in her throat, threatening to choke her, and crawled toward escape. When they'd gotten out of view, Davis tapped her shoulder and rushed to the left. She followed, grief and terror battling to pull her focus. She stumbled into Davis's back when he stopped on the backside of a wall tent pitched in a small clearing.

"I'm going to grab some gear." He shrugged off her

pack and helped her put it on like a child. "Stay here. Be ready to run."

She nodded, embarrassed that she couldn't seem to function beyond that. Davis buckled the strap around her waist, and, when her fingers fumbled with the chest strap, he clicked that closed as well. She grabbed at his fingers, her entire body shaking.

"Hey." He lifted her fingertips to his mouth and kissed them. "Trust me."

Her eyebrows drew together.

"Please." He closed his eyes for a second before piercing her with his determined, storm-gray gaze. "I'm not going to let them hurt you."

She swallowed and nodded. He was here. She wasn't in this alone.

"I'll be right back. Thirty seconds or less." Davis squeezed her fingers one last time and turned to the tent.

Her pulse increased as he undid the zipper in the middle of the tent's back panel, to the point she wanted to yank him to her and tell him to stop. She scanned the brush, waiting for the men to jump out. She was an idiot to think she ever compared to her siblings. All of this had her well and truly freaked out.

"Get it together, Rebel," Sunny whispered to herself, as Davis ducked into the tent.

She bit her bottom lip hard to gain control of her fear. When that didn't work to focus, she counted. When she reached fifteen, the sound of approaching footsteps shattered what little calm she'd gained. Davis hadn't had enough time.

Would he hear the man coming?

Should she warn him somehow?

The footsteps stopped, and a voice lifted from the other side of the tent. "What the—"

She reached her trembling fingers for the canvas just as Davis ducked out of the tent.

"Hey! We might have another problem." The man on the other side hollered back toward the cabin, and Davis quietly pulled the tent zipper closed

She wanted to throw her arms around Davis, but he signaled her to move through the willows. Not hesitating, she rushed quietly through the trees with at least enough sense to avoid the mud. Shouts rang from behind, and she pushed herself harder, desperate to get as far away as possible.

Chapter Twelve

NINE MONTHS Earlier

Day 3: Operation Fake Relationship for Lena's Wedding

Davis pulled at the jacket sleeves as he surveyed himself in the dressing room mirror on the men's side of the upscale wedding boutique. The expensive suit looked all right. Marshall, Lena's fiancé, wasn't sparing any expense, even though it was his second wedding. Davis rolled his neck and yanked at the collar.

A three-thousand-dollar suit was the most expensive he'd ever worn, and yet it felt…wrong.

Tight.

The entire situation of faking a relationship to keep his real purpose in Kentucky a secret choked him. Shoot, his whole life didn't fit him anymore. The more he tried to force himself into it, the more suffocated he felt.

He cleared his throat and closed his eyes, willing the anxiety that always buzzed along his skin to dissipate. It didn't work … nothing ever worked. The nervous energy would build and build until it finally overloaded him, and he would explode.

Deep laughter and joking from Lena's fiancé and others in the wedding party sounded from the opposite side of the thin door. The buzz skated up Davis's neck and spread to his shoulders. Another breath in and slowly out. He would not ruin Lena's wedding. She deserved this time to be full of happy memories, not worried that her friend, the one she was trusting to keep her stepson and sister safe, would blow.

The talking in the room shifted to calls of surprise. Davis snapped his eyes opened, his muscles tensing in anticipation of an attack. "Shhh," sounded among the voices followed by quick rapping on his dressing room door.

"Davis, you decent?" Sunny asked, then whispered loudly to the others. "You didn't just see me."

He swung open the door. "What's wrong?"

"Nothing." She pushed her way in and slammed the door. "I'm hiding."

The tension eased from his shoulders, and he leaned against the door. She held a to-go container with a large piece of cake in it. Her long, dark hair was haphazardly bundled in a knot on the top of her head. A gold dress draped over her tanned skin, making her look even more the goddess she normally was.

There was something about her that quieted the buzzing. He couldn't pinpoint what it was, even though he'd circled back to figuring her out repeatedly over the last three days they'd been in Kentucky together. He wanted to keep his distance, do the job, then get back to figuring out where he fit in with life. Yet, she kept leaning close, drawing him in, like they were co-conspirators or long-time friends, and he found himself not wanting to pull away.

She looked him up and down, patting his chest. "Nice. Not really you, but it'll do."

"What do you mean 'not really me'?" His forehead furrowed as she dug a plastic fork into the cake.

"I don't know. You just seem more the t-shirt and jeans type of guy. You know, more comfortable outside, working with your hands, than in a stuffy suit." She took a big bite of the cake, her eyes rolling in her head with a groan. "Oh, man. You've got to try this."

She forked him a bite and held it up to his lips. He held her gaze as he took the cake into his mouth. How could she think such a thing after barely knowing him? And why did her simple assessment of him fit better than any others he could come up with?

"Delicious, right?" She smiled up at him with an easy-going manner and something hard shifted inside him.

"Pretty good." In truth, he hadn't really tasted it.

"Sunniva Rebel, are you in here?" Sunny's mom hollered into the room.

"Oh, nuts." Sunny climbed onto the chair in the corner of the dressing room and ducked her head. "I'm not here."

She wobbled, and Davis stepped close, placing his hand on her waist to steady her. She giggled, then pressed her lips together to keep quiet. Her effervescence bubbled over him, and he shrugged against the unfamiliar sensation.

"Why aren't you here?" His whisper came out low and hoarse.

"I'm not trying on one more dress." She braced her

hand on his shoulder and leaned so her breath tickled her ear. "They always joke about Bridezilla, but Mom's turned into Momzilla, and all her focus is on me today."

"Why's that?" Davis asked, looking up at Sunny.

"Who knows." Her expression shifted, and the brightness shining from her dimmed. "Probably doesn't think I'll make the right choice…again."

He didn't like seeing her sadness. He doubted Sunny's mom meant to single Sunny out. He'd over-heard her talking to her husband about how she just wanted the wedding to be perfect for Lena. That didn't mean her actions hadn't hurt Sunny's feelings.

"Don't worry. You're safe with me. Momzilla will never know you're here." He dropped his whisper even lower as Sunny's mom started questioning the guys in the room.

The smile Sunny gave him slid warmth under his skin and deep into his cells. He nodded and turned toward the door, needing space to clear his thoughts. He slowed his rush into the bigger room to intercept Momzilla so he didn't look like he was running away. In truth, he didn't know what to do with Sunny, run away or draw closer. The fact that he didn't know scared him.

Davis stumbled behind Sunny through the undergrowth. Alaska had to be the most frustrating terrain to navigate, with its permafrost marshes and moss that sucked his foot in and tripped him up. It made him miss Colorado's high-desert mountains, where he could hike forever with no issue.

"Come on! I think she's this way." A yell from

behind pushed him to stretch his legs farther, terrain or not.

Davis had hoped for a bigger lead, but nothing had gone in their favor. Sunny didn't look back, just plowed forward. He kept an eye on her trail, glad at least the horrible terrain mostly covered their tracks.

She'd recovered from her teeter on the edge of breaking down. He didn't blame her. This was her first experience with such evil. He'd almost blown it back there too. If it hadn't been for her stopping him, he'd probably be tossed in the burning cabin with Justin.

Davis shook the thought away. He just needed her to continue believing that he could keep her safe. Having her trust burned away everything else. He'd seen the doubt in her eyes. Had she heard the desperation in his voice when he'd practically begged her to have faith in him? The vulnerability left him exposed, and he didn't like it.

He glanced behind and caught a swath of color through the brush about three hundred yards back. The men gained ground. If Davis didn't come up with something, and fast, his and Sunny's position would be completely blown.

Why had he let his guard down around camp and not carried a sidearm? They kept a rifle at the cabin that they'd take to the mine site just in case an animal wandered too close, but he hadn't used it since he got there. It had helped ease his stress-level not carrying a weapon all the time, always looking for danger.

Stupid move. He'd buried his handgun so deep in his gear stashed in his totes, he hadn't been able to find it when he needed it most. Now he had nothing but his hands and what he found in nature to protect Sunny with. And those only worked if the men chasing them got close enough.

He peeked back and stumbled when Sunny grabbed his hand and yanked him off course. Jerking his attention to their front, he scanned for whatever danger she'd seen. Nothing was there but an overgrown trail barely discernible in the thick moss.

A branch jabbed him in the neck as Sunny barreled into the thick brush, dragging him with her. She let go of his hand and crawled through the tangled branches. This was a bad idea. Shouldn't they keep moving fast, not creep through bushes?

He stopped short when the branches opened to a small half-circle at the base of a cluster of black spruce. In the middle was an old ladder tied to a handful of trees with frayed rope. Sunny scampered up the ladder, the rungs creaking with each step.

Davis tipped his head up, his eyes widening in shock. Two partial plywood sheets hid among the branches. She reached the first one, tested its stability, then climbed on.

Why was that even there, and how did she know it was?

Her head popped over the side, and she waved him up. He glanced back toward the men. Their loud rush through the forest probably meant they hadn't actually seen Sunny. That or they didn't care enough to keep quiet.

Why would they? The only ones around to hear them were Sunny and Davis. And if their noise pushed their prey along, eventually Davis or Sunny would make a mistake.

"Psst." Her noise barely made it down to him.

He peered up. She pulled her eyebrows together and jerked her head, motioning him to get up there. Was that the right move?

He surveyed the small space and the brush around the trees. If he stayed below, he could keep anyone else from going up. But, if they saw him, they could just put a bullet through his chest from outside the brush and then climb up anyway. Maybe having the higher vantage point would be smart. Most people never looked up.

"Psst." Sunny's call hissed more insistently down at him.

If he didn't join her on the platform, she'd probably come down for him. So much for him being at the helm. Didn't matter. She'd found a place to hide. Hopefully, hiding was the right option.

Chapter Thirteen

Nine Months Earlier

Day 7: Fake Relationship with a Real-Life Hero

Sunny scanned the guests at the reception, soaking in the joy that saturated the atmosphere. She sighed as Marshall held Lena close as they danced, her sister's cheeks pinking at whatever her new husband whispered in her ear. No two people deserved happiness more than them.

"That will be you soon, sweetheart. I promise." Marshall's grandma bumped Sunny's shoulder with a chuckle.

"Oh, I don't think so." Sunny shook her head, trying not to let her own lack infiltrate the happiness.

"I've seen the way your young man looks at you."

"Davis?" Sunny stifled her laugh at the thought of the distant man pretending to be her boyfriend looking at her lovingly.

She had to watch what she said since only a few select people knew their relationship was fake.

"With the way he watches you like there's nothing else in the world worth looking at, I'd say you'll be walking down your own aisle sooner than you think." The old woman winked, then pointed her chin toward Davis standing off to the side of the crowd.

Sure enough, his gaze locked with Sunny's. Marshall's grandma cackled as she patted Sunny's shoulder in a told-you-so way and walked off. Crazy old woman. Why do people always see love where there was none? Maybe it was human delusion, this hope that everyone would find their happily ever after.

Davis's eyebrow rose and lips lifted on one side as he made his way across the reception area to Sunny. She jerked her gaze away, too late realizing she'd been staring at him. Her eyes didn't stray long, though, as he confidently strode toward her.

"Care to dance?" His sultry, low voice oozed like melted rich, dark chocolate over her, tempting her to rise up on her toes and taste his words.

"I'd love to." Giddiness flooded her as he threaded his fingers through hers and lead her to the dance floor.

They'd already danced several times, and Davis Fields, her robot, fake boyfriend, had moves. His country swing, while stiff, had pleasantly surprised her, keeping her guessing what he'd do next. She'd been glad for Lena's warning, otherwise his aloofness during the week would have stung. Instead, the mystery of who Davis was before he'd changed intrigued Sunny.

He lifted her hand over her head and twirled her, then pulled her close against him. She closed her eyes and inhaled a deep breath of his earthy cologne. It reminded her of being outdoors, but sexier.

"You okay?" He whispered in her ear, sending a shiver of delight down her spine.

"Yeah. Why?"

"It looked like whatever Gamma Suzy said upset you." He skimmed his fingers against the bare skin of her back.

"Gamma?" Sunny chuckled, but it came out breathless. She couldn't focus with his calloused skin smoothing along hers.

He shrugged. "She insisted I call her that. She's … a character."

"She's cute." Sunny pulled him closer, running her fingers into the hair along his neck.

He flinched, and she almost pulled away. Then, he spread his hands wide on her back, pushing her flush against him with a growl.

"Firefly, you've got me on dangerous ground here." He pressed a kiss to the place where her shoulder and neck met.

Hope blasted her off into the air, then excitement's thrusters rocketed her even higher. Could Gamma Suzy's observation be real? Sunny's heart raced as he held her close through the rest of the dance into the next.

▭

Sunny cringed as the ladder groaned with each of Davis's steps up. She shifted on the flaking plywood and bit her lip when it creaked. Maybe this old tree stand wasn't the best place to hide out. From the way the boards peeled upwards, they had been nailed up here for a long time.

Davis's palm pressed to the wood a second before his head popped into view. She backed up against the trunks of two trees, their spindly branches jabbing her through her jacket. When Davis hefted himself up on the board, she squeezed her eyes shut, waiting for it to crash down.

The platform was small, barely big enough for the two of them. Davis's pack pushed against her as he adjusted. She pulled her knees to her chest to give him more space. With his one arm pressed against her shin and his pack against her side, he froze.

She held her breath, scanning below them for their pursuers. Davis tipped his head like an owl, then motioned with his hands that he had eyes on them. Sunny bit her lip and looked the direction Davis was watching. The willows waved like signal flags, marking the men's approach. If only Davis had some kind of weapon.

Wait a minute. She sat up a little straighter, angry at herself. *Sunny, you are an idiot.*

Slowly, she reached back to her pack and pulled her bear gun from the hidden pocket. Why hadn't she thought of it before? Her family would blow a fuse when they found out. She'd just keep that part of the story out when they got home.

If they got home.

Tapping Davis on the arm, she held the gun out to him when he turned his attention to her. His lips arched up and appreciation beamed from his eyes. He silently slid the magazine out, checked the load, and eased it back in.

"Ammo?" He whispered the question.

She pulled the two spare magazines from the side

pocket of her pack, gritting her teeth and holding her breath when the movement rattled the spruces's branches. Opening her palm to Davis, she shrugged and mouthed, "That's it." He nodded and curled her fingers around the magazines.

"Do you think we'll catch up to her?" The shooter's voice broke the quiet of the forest, causing a squirrel to chatter angrily.

"You better hope we do," his partner growled back.

"You don't think Zhang would actually kill us." The tremble in the shooter's laugh showed his nervousness.

"I'm just glad he didn't shoot us right there and burn our bodies with the miner's." The second man stopped below the tree stand and ran his hand through his hair before shoving his hat back on. "Though he probably would just toss us in the woods and let the wolves and bears take care of us. Less evidence that way."

"Dude, not cool."

Sunny could see the shooter's face through the thick brush and branches. He had his eyes open so wide they looked like they'd pop out. The other man pointed his gun at the shooter. Sunny held her breath, wanting to close her eyelids just in case. She didn't think she could handle watching someone else get shot.

"What's not cool is you not taking care of the girl in the first place and putting us on Zhang's radar. Now she has help, and if we don't find them, we're both dead." He shoved his gun in his holster and squatted.

"We don't know if she has help or not." The shooter shook his head as his partner scanned the ground. "Whoever's tent that is could have gone to town. Shoot, it could be her tent, for all we know. If it's someone else's, he'll get back and find just a burned up shell and his friend's remains."

"Maybe. We can't assume anything since we thought Justin Freedom was mining alone." The partner stood and tossed a leaf down. "Even if she doesn't have help, she's good in the woods. I can't pick up her trail." He cursed and kicked at the moss. "I can't track in this stuff."

She shouldn't feel bolstered by the evil man's comment, but she was. If they got caught, it wouldn't be from her inexperience. She smiled at the knowledge the man just gave her, but it quickly morphed into a grimace as a searing cramp shot up her thigh and back.

She smashed her lips together and gritted her teeth. The pain increased. She needed to adjust her position. If she moved, the men would hear. There was no way they wouldn't, not with them standing right below the tree stand. Her breath shuddered as she inhaled, and she squeezed her eyes closed as a tear rushed out. Of all the times to have her muscle spasm, this had to be the worst.

Davis touched her foot, and her eyes popped open.

"You okay?" he mouthed.

She lifted her shoulders a fraction and silently replied, "Muscle cramp."

He nodded, his eyebrows V-ing together in concern as he did a quick scan of her before focusing back on the men. He slowly leaned more into her, tucking her leg between his arm and body. She hid her smile against her knees. Davis really was just a big ol' cinnamon roll— crusty on the outside, but warm and sweet on the inside.

To distract herself from the men still arguing below, and her body rebelling in pain, she thought back to the time she'd spent with Davis in Kentucky. He wasn't a part of Lena's regular security team, so Lena had set it up that Davis pretend to be Sunny's boyfriend there for the wedding and to help her babysit after. Sunny hadn't complained, since the man was hotter than an Alaskan wildfire. After an awkward week before the wedding, she and Davis even had fun at the reception, dancing most of the night away under the Kentucky stars.

Sunny's cheeks heated as she remembered the way he'd held her while they'd danced. The touch of his palm burned against the bare skin her low-backed dress exposed. He'd pulled her close, his lips skimming her ear as he whispered words that had made the air thin like she was on top of the world again.

"Firefly, you've got me on dangerous ground here."

Opening her eyes, she leaned her cheek on her knees and stared at Davis's profile. He never told her why he called her that. She hadn't cared, not when he said it like a caress. He'd been so professional the entire week leading up to the wedding, holding hands and staying close to her for appearance's sake, but remaining distant. The change at the reception had pleasantly surprised her and led to the best two weeks she'd had in a long, long time.

Then…nothing.

Ghosted.

The pain moved from her leg to her heart. What was it about her that made men disappear? She didn't think she was annoying. Cheerful, yes, but not in the irritating way.

"They're gone." Davis sighed low and hugged her leg to him. "You okay?"

No. Not really, but she wouldn't tell him that.

"Yeah." She forced a smile and stretched her leg out. "Felt like a bear had gripped my back and tried to pull me apart."

"Ouch. Let me take your pack. That should help." He grabbed the straps, and she unbuckled it. "I want to stay up here for a bit, make sure they don't double back on us."

"Okay. We can probably put our packs on that other piece of plywood." She pointed to the smaller platform a foot above their heads.

He pulled on it. When it held, he hefted her pack up, then shrugged out of his. He opened it and pulled a worn, dark green sweatshirt from inside, then set the bag next to hers.

"How did you even see this?" he asked as he yanked the sweatshirt over his head.

"It looked like what my dad builds around his bear stations. I just kind of hoped there'd be space to hide once we got inside. Lucky us, it came with a tree stand." She patted the wood, then cringed when a splinter jabbed into her palm. "Oh!"

"Here, let me."

Davis cradled the back of her hand in his palm and gently pulled the splinter out. He rubbed his thumb over the bead of blood, her pulse hitching at his gentleness. She held her breath as she waited to see what he'd do next. When he set her hand on her leg, she barely stopped the roll of her eyes at her disappointment in him not kissing it better. She had definitely read too many romance novels over the winter.

She shifted around, stretching her leg out. The board was just too small to get comfortable sitting side by side like they were. She scanned the trees holding the plywood up and picked two that looked like a good back rest.

"If we're hanging out up here a while, let's at least try to get comfortable." She stood, leaning over Davis's head in the cramped space, and snapped all the branches from the two trees. "Move forward a little."

When he did, she sat behind him, stretching her legs out on both sides of him. She leaned back against the trees. Not the most comfortable, but not horrible. Davis stretched his back, and she grabbed his sweatshirt and pulled on it.

"Skootch on back."

The contrary man shook his head. "I'm fine. Need to stay on lookout."

"Why do you think I'm back here?"

The military sure knew how to cultivate heroism in their Special Forces. He was so much like her brothers she could practically hear them saying the exact same thing.

"Come on, Davis. I've got this nice back rest. You can lean against me so your muscles don't kink up, and still scan for bad guys."

He peeked back at her, so she patted the spot right in front of her.

"Fine." He sighed and moved against her. "But only because I can shield you better this way."

He didn't lean against her, his body staying rigid. She closed her eyes, pushing the hurt aside that he held himself away. She wasn't surviving alone anymore. That's all that mattered.

"I'm so scared," she whispered, not caring if it made her seem weak.

He sighed and relaxed against her. "Me too, Firefly. Me too"

She leaned her head on his shoulder, turned her face into his neck, and smiled. Putting too much stock in that moment wouldn't be smart. Yet, as she wrapped her arms around him and let his solid presence warm her, the emptiness she'd held for so long didn't seem so cavernous.

Chapter Fourteen

AFTER AN HOUR OF JOGGING, Davis slowed to a walk. They'd put a lot of distance between the tree stand and them, but he still had this inner warning to get as far as possible fast. Good thing the Alaskan summer nights never got pitch black. Even though the day pushed past midnight, the sun's glow was enough to trek without using a flashlight that could give their location away.

He peeked back at Sunny. Her cheeks were red from exertion, and her chest heaved, but she hadn't complained about the pace he set. Hadn't fallen behind either.

Scanning the forest before him, he narrowed his eyes at the dark clouds building on the horizon. The last thing they needed was more rain, especially if it stormed. Finding a campsite just became top priority.

Sunny sniffed behind him, and he stifled the urge to make sure she was all right. She didn't need or probably want him coddling her. Shoot, she was tougher than most people he knew, with her repeated summits up the world's tallest mountains and her expedition to the North Pole.

"What the heck is going on, Davis? Who are these men?" She kept her voice low, even though he was pretty sure they were miles away from the enemy.

"They are from an exploratory mining company located a few miles from the homestead." He adjusted his pack and took off across the edge of a ridge.

"That doesn't make a lick of sense." Sunny huffed out.

He wished he knew more, but he was as confused by all of this as she was.

"All I know is they've been wanting to buy Justin out. He went over there this morning to tell them not under any circumstance would he sell his family's mine." Was that only that morning?

"But—" Her voice hitched on a sob. "Why kill Justin? What could possibly be worth murdering over?"

Davis stopped and hung his head.

"I mean, even with Justin dead, they won't be able to just come in and claim his mine." Sunny's voice got thinner and thinner the more she talked.

Davis turned to her, his heart falling at the agony splotching her face a mixture of ashy skin and red. He stepped up to her and slipped his hand to the nape of her neck. He wanted to fix this, to take her away from here so she wouldn't have this weight for the rest of her life. Violence like she'd witnessed couldn't be forgotten.

"Hey."

She spoke over him, clutching her fingers around his forearm. "Justin had been so excited to be at the homestead again. I mean, I hadn't seen him that happy in a long time."

"I didn't know you knew him." Davis rubbed his thumb across her cheek, wondering how their connection had slipped past him.

"Our families have been friends for years. My parents grew up with his dad." Her words became frantic and garbled with her crying. "I used to play with Justin every summer we came to the Fortymile district. His family would hunt with us for a few weeks in the fall before they went down to their winter home in Homer. We pretended to be soldiers scouting the woods. He … he—"

Her voice broke along with a piece of Davis's heart.

"Hey, shh." He wrapped her in his arms and held her close. "They won't get away with this. I promise."

She buried her face against his neck, her entire body jerking with her sobs. His own grief welled up within, but he pushed it down, letting it harden into anger. No matter what the cost, even if he had to go rogue, he'd make sure the men and company paid for what they did to Justin and to Sunny.

Eye for an eye. Wasn't that the saying?

He closed his eyes and inhaled the faint scent of Sunny's citrus shampoo. Sliding his fingers through her silky hair, he let the feel against his skin soothe him. He couldn't feed into the anger, not now when he needed to keep Sunny safe. Needed to comfort her.

Swallowing against the lie clogging his throat, he chided himself. If he couldn't be honest with himself, he was more doomed than he thought. The truth was, he needed the comfort as much as she did.

The next few minutes, he took that solace, running his fingers rhythmically through her hair and letting her presence cool him. Hadn't that been the enigma of her in the first place? When he'd helped her watch Lena and Marshall's son, he'd found a sense of serenity just being around Sunny. It was like she had calmed the fire in him, which was just plain dumb, since he'd felt heat just with a smile from her.

"Why didn't you tell me you were up here?" Sunny tipped her head to see him.

Her red-rimmed, dark brown eyes popped with the gold that streaked from her irises. Hurt laced her words, jabbing him in the heart. He'd wanted to call her, wanted to chase after her when she'd left Kentucky. Instead, he'd tucked tail and hid back in Colorado, ignoring her texts and calls until they stopped all together.

He stared down at her, wanting to hedge from this discussion. Her bottom lip trembled, and she bit it. He couldn't hide from her anymore, not if he wanted her to trust him.

"I'd … I'd been in a hard place." He pulled his hand through her hair, watching the strands slide over his rough skin. "Still am, if I'm honest. All I did was upset those around me. It's just … I mean, I didn't think being around people was smart until I figured things out, especially someone who shines as bright as you do." He sucked up some courage and looked her in the eyes. "I couldn't risk hurting you."

"Okay." She licked her lips, then leaned her forehead against his collarbone with a sigh.

What?

No more questions?

Davis's forehead scrunched in confusion as she took another deep breath and wrapped her arms around his waist. Maybe, with her siblings and dad ex-military,

Sunny had a better understanding of the effects of PTSD than most. Hope flickered in his heart like a jar full of fireflies. She called to him, blinking a way out of the darkness he couldn't seem to climb out of on his own.

Chapter Fifteen

Sunny's entire body ached with exhaustion, like letting her tears free also emptied her of what strength she had left. Thunder rumbled low, quickening her heart. It wasn't often that they'd get thunderstorms up there in the Alaskan Interior. When they did, it either meant wildfires or downpours. Neither would be good at the moment.

"We need to find shelter." Davis scanned the sky, then the forest ahead of them.

"Yep." She didn't know what else to say.

She was too tired to even think at the moment, though his earlier words about why he hadn't called sure seemed to not have any problem replaying in her head. Shaking out her hands to wake herself up, she surveyed the area they were in. Being on the top of the ridge should help them find some place not a soaking marsh. However, if it rained, there wouldn't be anywhere dry. A section of older spruce up ahead caught her eye.

"Davis, let's go check out that area." She stepped up

next to him when he stopped, and pointed to the mature trees.

"Good idea." He nodded, then extended his hand. "Lead the way."

She smiled over at him. Even with all his military training, he was letting her take the lead. Her exhaustion couldn't keep down the thrill his action brought.

Searching the terrain for the perfect shelter was always difficult in Alaska. Many of the trees, especially the black spruce, were too spindly to provide any protection or grew so thick one couldn't get between them. Add how the ground could be solid one moment and marshy, uneven ickiness the next didn't help. Permafrost sure knew how to cause problems. Thankfully, this area was free of it, and the spruce grew tall.

She spotted a decent black spruce ahead and made a beeline for it. The height wasn't as tall as some others, which would be good if the thunder rumbling meant lightning storm, but the branches grew thick and wide. She rubbed her foot at the ground beneath, glad to find dirt and spruce needles rather than wet moss.

"This should work," she said, just as the clouds opened up.

She grabbed her collapsible saw from her pack, then tossed the bag up against the trunk of the tree. If they didn't want to get rained on all night, they'd have to reinforce what the tree had. Davis set his pack next to hers, then turned to her expectantly.

"I'm going to cut some boughs from the other trees." She clicked open her saw and pointed her chin at the closest spruce.

"Good. I'll get the ground ready." Davis ducked under their shelter's branches and got to work.

What? No fight over the more laborious job? With the way her shoulders ached, she might even give in, but she loved that he knew she could handle it. She rolled her neck and got to work.

She cut branch after branch off of the neighboring spruces, chucking them into a pile near their shelter. The pelting rain made the saw slippery and increased her frustration. Davis worked just as hard, running down the slope repeatedly and coming back with armfuls of birch leaves for their bed. In the back of her mind, she worried about leaving so much evidence of their location, but it couldn't be helped.

When she had a good pile of branches, she picked out the smallest ones and threaded them in among their spruce's own. Davis helped, working from a few feet away. When they got too high for her to reach, she let Davis continue and shifted her focus on weaving the larger boughs into a front wall.

Davis soon joined her, their hands brushing occasionally as they wove. They didn't speak, just worked, anticipating what each other would need. She knew it was because of his military training and her own wilderness background, but it had to mean something that they worked so well together. Right?

"Let's see if we've got enough." Sunny lifted one side and waited until Davis grabbed the other.

They fitted it up against the bottom limbs of their shelter. She snatched a couple of zip ties from her pocket and secured the wall to the tree. It probably didn't need it, but she wanted to be sure it wouldn't get ripped off if the wind picked up.

She wiped rain off her face, wishing it would just give them a break, and stepped back to survey their work. "I think that should be good enough. Let me check inside." She kneeled down and peeked her head through the small opening they'd kept. "It's dry."

"Climb on in, and I'll just put these leftover branches above us." Davis touched the small of her back, rushing the chill from the rain away in a whoosh, before his feet squelched through the mud to the last branches.

She crawled in to the farthest side, more than happy to be done for the day. Pulling her pack into her lap, she rifled through it, setting the items they'd need for the night aside. It wasn't much, some food, water, and her sleeping bag. She clicked on her headlamp and hung it from a branch. Their reinforcing job made it dark inside. She mentally cataloged the food that she had and calculated how long it would last between the two of them.

Not long.

Definitely not enough to get them to civilization.

Davis crawled in, and she quickly zipped her pack and set it aside. They'd just have to worry about that later. They had more pressing things to worry about than lack of grub, like homicidal people chasing them. She could scavenge the land for food when they ran out.

"Well, this is cozy." Davis's low voice curled warmth in her stomach.

"At least it's not wet." A gust of wind pelted rain against the branch wall and made her shiver. "Too bad we won't be able to start a fire and dry out."

"You have a change of clothes, right?" Davis wiped at the water dripping from his hair.

"Yeah."

"Good. We need to strip out of these soggy things."

His words shouldn't make her blush, especially with how used to close quarters she was with her treks up Mount Denali with mostly men, but it did. "I covered a section behind me so our clothes can dry out overnight. Well, at least not be soaked."

She nodded, hoping he couldn't see her blush in the dim light. When he cleared his throat, she glanced up from digging in her pack. His ears burned red, and his eyes darted to her, then away.

"I'll just turn around." He shifted in the small space so his back was to her.

Her cheeks hurt from her smile. How could this warrior be embarrassed over something like this? She bit her lip, turned her back to him, and quickly swapped clothes.

She really wasn't sure what to do with him, with the words he'd confessed. Sure, they hadn't been in a rela-tionship or anything, but him ghosting her had hurt. She figured it was because of her, but, if she could believe what he said earlier, his reason for not contacting her soothed her bruised heart.

"Done?" He cleared his throat again.

"Yeah." She zipped up her fleece jacket, glad she'd had it in her pack.

"Hand me your clothes."

Their fingers brushed, and she shivered at the contact. His eyebrows V-ed on his forehead, and his lips pressed tightly together. His concern made her smile. She'd led mountaineers up Denali for so long that it'd been a while since someone worried about her. Gunnar had, on their trek to the North Pole, but that was the annoying, overbearing brother kind of worry. Davis's care wasn't irritating at all.

"We need to get warm." He hung the clothes from branches, his back to her as he mumbled, "The last thing we need is hypothermia along with murderers."

And just like that, the terror of the day had her teeth chattering. She reached into her pack, her hand quivering, and grabbed her sleeping bag. As she laid it out in the small space, she cringed at the mummy bag. She loved her Mountain Hard Wear Phantom, but it definitely wasn't meant for two people.

"Did you grab a sleeping bag from your tent?" She glanced at his pack, wondering for the first time what he was able to pack.

He shook his head and huffed out a disgusted grunt. "I only had time to get clothes and the few packaged food items I had in the tent before I heard the footsteps. I stupidly thought the Alaskan wilderness was a place I could finally relax. A place to stop being paranoid that someone was going to jump out of the shadows or that I'd have to bug out. My pack was shoved under my cot, empty, and most of our supplies were in the cabin with the computer."

"It's okay. I never thought this would happen here, either." She swallowed.

"Yeah, well, I should've known better." He clenched his teeth.

A shiver ran through her. "Well, that just means I'll warm up faster with us sharing. I shouldn't be this cold, not after the expedition to the North Pole, but I can't stop shaking."

"Climb in." Davis nudged her shoulder. "I'll take the zipper side."

The cold side. She nodded and slid into the bag with her back to Davis. Would they both even fit? He turned off her headlamp, plunging them into darkness, and slipped in. He hesitated a moment before his arm wrapped around her waist and pulled her close.

"You know, for a mummy bag, this thing has decent foot space." He shifted his legs so his feet cradled the bottom of hers.

"It has extra room down there for gear you don't want to freeze. Worked great on the expedition." She tried to relax her muscles, but she couldn't with him so close.

"I enjoyed the videos you posted about the expedition. You made it feel like I was right there with you." His low words shot through her.

"My camera." She tried to sit up, but the space was too tight. "I had my GoPro on when I walked into your camp."

"Leave it for now."

"But—"

"It's not going anywhere, and watching it now won't help us." He adjusted his position, pulling the sleeping bag closed tighter.

Relief crashed over her. She didn't think she could handle watching it at the moment, and she hated herself for that weakness. In the morning, she'd watch it, whether or not she could handle it. Justin deserved that much, deserved his murderers brought to justice.

As she slowed her breathing and relaxed a little into Davis's hold, his words jolted through her again. He'd enjoyed her videos? Why would he even bother when he'd left her hanging?

"You really watched?" she whispered, then held her breath, waiting for his response.

"Yeah. I watched them all." His swallow was loud in

her ear. "I've watched all of your videos. Might have even downloaded them to my phone."

He laughed it off, but she heard the truth of the confession in his tone.

"Why?"

Why would he download her videos, but not call, text, or email? Nothing.

"Because they … you make life brighter." He groaned and buried his face into the space between her neck and the sleeping bag. "Now, I sound like some kind of stalker."

She didn't know what to do with that. Was he being honest with her or just playing her? Her tendency was to see the good in people. It was incredibly naïve and had stripped everything from her. Her money, her job, her confidence. Nevertheless, being on guard wasn't in her nature. She was just too gullible, which was why she figured being by herself would keep her safe from emotional hurt. She could live with the gaping hole of loneliness solitude left in her, couldn't she?

No. No, she really couldn't. This last adventure taught her that.

She rolled over, grunting and shifting awkwardly in the tight space.

"Sunny—*oomph*." Davis's breath rushed out as she accidentally elbowed him in the gut. "What are you doing?"

"Sorry." She giggled as their legs tangled together, and she sputtered as her hair escaping her braid got in her mouth. "I just—"

She sighed, not knowing what to say. Her knowledge of this man could fill a teaspoon, and yet … she wanted to believe that what he'd said earlier was true. That he had worried about hurting her and that was why he hadn't called. Didn't him downloading her videos contradict his not contacting her?

"Sunny?" He brushed her wild hair from her face, shifting to give her more space.

She didn't care if she was naïve, gullible, or just plain dumb. Having Davis here, knowing he cared enough to keep her show on his phone, cinched that hole of loneliness closed a bit. Not all the way, but enough that she could breathe a little easier than before.

She leaned forward in the dark and pressed her lips to his. He smelled of rain and spruce. He froze like a snowshoe hare just noticing danger. His heart pounded fast against her palms pressed to his chest. She smiled at how both their pulses raced.

Kissing him one more time, she whispered against his lips, "I'm so glad you're here with me." She sighed and snuggled into him, pressing her cheek against his collarbone and pulling close to him. "You make me feel safe, cared for."

"I want to protect you." He tucked his chin on her head and pulled her tightly to him like any minute someone would rip her away. "I just don't know if I can."

She shook her head. "I trust you."

She did?

Searching into her heart, the statement held.

Healed.

"You shouldn't." His barely whispered words plinked like ice cubes in her gut.

She squeezed her eyes shut to the doubt that chilled her.

Chapter Sixteen

Nine Months Earlier

Day 17: Operation Fake Relationship for Lena's Wedding

Davis watched Sunny's fingers as they trailed through Carter's hair. His mouth hung open, and soft snores were a contrast to his normal chattiness. The five-year-old had run them so hard all day, he'd finally fallen asleep with his head in Sunny's lap while they watched fireflies in the backyard. The fire they'd roasted marshmallows in for s'mores burned low and was more coals than flames.

"Want me to put him in the tent?" Davis asked.

He marveled again at how good at this Sunny was. Her suggestion to go camping in the backyard had been a hit, just like all her other ideas to keep Carter entertained.

"Nah, I'll hold him a little bit longer." Sunny's soft smile as she gazed lovingly at her nephew thickened Davis's throat with longing.

Longing to be at peace in any situation like she was.

Maybe even longing to have a family of his own.

To have a future.

Davis, on the other hand, felt more confused than ever. In the week and a half since Lena and Marshall had left on their honeymoon, the stress of staying on guard had crawled along his skin. But then there were times like this one, when all the edginess and worry and anger disappeared.

"Just a few more days and it's back to reality." Sunny's disappointed words rushed his PTSD back to the surface.

He didn't want reality.

He hated it.

But he couldn't also have this, not without getting his issues under control. He tore his gaze from her and stared into the fire.

"What's next for you?" He knew she was a world-renowned mountaineer, but, aside from a few comments here and there, they hadn't talked about life outside of Kentucky.

They'd existed in this bubble, the fake morphing until it felt real. He knew the alter-reality where happiness existed couldn't last. He'd let himself escape into it more than he ever thought he could.

"Back to Alaska and preparing for winter." She cringed. "I'm spending the season stuck in a cabin in Chicken with Gunnar, training for a dog sledding expedition to the North Pole we probably won't even take."

He'd heard of Chicken. His friend Justin gold mined north of there and wanted Davis to come help him the next summer. At first, going had felt like running away from his responsibilities to the team at Stryker and his family. Now, after this time with Sunny, he wondered if the Alaskan wilderness was what he needed to finally heal.

"Why won't you go to the North Pole?"

"We're just alternates for the expedition. So, the likelihood of us actually going is slim." She shrugged. "But the organizer is paying us to mush dogs all winter in some of the most beautiful country in the world, so I can't complain too much. As long as my cranky brother doesn't drive me crazy, it'll be like an extended vacation."

"Not sure my sister would want to be stuck with me in a cabin all winter." Davis shook his head. "She'd probably kill me."

"Yeah. I'm a little worried about that myself." Sunny laughed then penetrated him with her gaze. "What about you? Off to protect someone exciting?"

"No. I think—" He snapped his mouth shut against the words that wanted out.

He needed to just push them down like every other time they tried to give voice. He swallowed, but they stuck to his tongue, pushing against the seam of his lips.

"Davis?"

Sunny laid her hand on his arm, concern thick in his name. His eyes trailed from her hand to her face. Her eyebrows V'ed over her dark eyes, and the words broke past his resistance and tumbled free.

"I think I'm done at Stryker." He took a deep breath, his chest finally free of the massive invisible weight the decision had on him. "That's not what I want in life anymore."

"Oh? What will you do?" There wasn't any criticism on her face, just interest.

"I'm not sure—at least long term. My friend wants

me to help him at his mine in Alaska. Being away from everything seems like a good idea."

"If you come to Alaska, we'll have to get together." Sunny's shy smile warmed his skin.

"I'd like that."

Her smile widened. "I wouldn't be opposed to keeping in touch once we are back in reality."

He took a deep breath. "I'd like that, too."

She bit her bottom lip, squeezed his arm, then released it to push Carter's hair off his forehead. "We should probably get settled in the tent. This guy will be ready to go full force as soon as the sun is up."

"Yeah."

"Here, can you let these fireflies loose?" Sunny handed him the jar blinking with insects they'd helped Carter catch earlier. "I don't want to accidentally suffocate them."

He stared at the jar as her words took root. Davis's hands trembled as he opened the lid. Sunny's light was just like these fireflies. Could he really keep in contact with her? Keep the hope he had flickering in his chest like the bugs—hope for a future not always needing to look over his shoulder, a future full of sunshine instead of darkness? Or would he end up squashing that hope, squashing her, just like he'd ruined so much else in his life?

***

Davis trailed behind Sunny as she led the way to Chicken. It was miles away and would take them days to get to. At least the rain had let up, but not before the storm the night before had raged and beat against their shelter.

Their too cozy shelter.

Holding Sunny in his arms through the night had all kinds of crazy thoughts spinning through his head. Ones of home and hope. Elusive dreams of marriage and peace. The last one pushed a snort of laughter out of him. How could he be thinking of peace when they were being hunted down by madmen?

Sunny turned to him and raised her eyebrow. "You okay?"

"Yeah, just woolgathering." Davis scanned the forest for signs of danger.

Thank goodness the downpour had washed away any trail he and Sunny had left. They might have a chance to get to safety and the authorities now. Hopefully, once Sunny's camera recharged with her portable charger, they'd have the evidence needed to put the murderers behind bars.

His gaze dragged back to Sunny. He'd done that too many times in the hours they'd been hiking through the day. He needed to keep his focus on the surroundings, not the woman who made his heart race with possibilities.

"Woolgathering?" The laughter in her voice tempted him to smile. "I don't think I've ever heard anyone use that phrase before." She peeked back at him as she stepped over a downed tree, an impish grin on her face. "At least, not anyone under sixty."

"Funny." He rolled his eyes and steadied her when her boot lace snagged on the black spruce branch.

He really hated trekking through this arctic forest.

One was either fighting with the thick spindly spruce or bogging through muskeg. Neither was fun. Hopefully, they could find another dry area with bigger trees like they had the night before, when it came time to make camp.

"Thanks." She huffed a sigh that smelled of the LemonHead candy she'd shared with him earlier, placed her hands on her head, and stretched. "Ugh. This is such slow going."

"Yep."

She unhooked her water bottle from her pack and took a drink. He grunted a thanks when she extended it to him and tried to ignore her stare. Taking his time to drink, he scanned behind them again.

"So … woolgathering, huh?" She grabbed the bottle from him, her fingers lingering on his longer than necessary.

"Yep." He schooled his smile when she huffed in frustration.

"What has you using old lady phrases?"

Sunny adjusted her pack on her shoulders. Could he convince her to transfer more of her gear to his? He'd tried to take most of the heavier gear, but she'd growled adorably, claiming she didn't need pampering. True. She was stronger than any other woman he'd ever met, and he'd served with some amazing women. Shoot, she could outperform most of the men he knew too. Didn't mean his desire to make things easier on her didn't scream at him every time she winced or rolled her neck.

"Nothing, just thinking," he answered her question when she tipped her head at him.

He wanted to open his mouth and let all the thoughts churning in his head spew. She drew him to want the unattainable, to believe he could grasp a life full of joy instead of dread. He just wasn't sure he could trust his intuition anymore. Last time he had, he'd gotten half his team killed.

Granted, Sunny wasn't an enemy combatant posing as an attention-starved teenage boy.

More like Davis himself was the imposter, someone who couldn't be trusted. Someone who would snap and destroy everything good and beautiful around him. Would he smother the light that burned Sunny brighter than others?

"That really clears it up." Sunny stomped off. "No worries. I'm used to reticent men who grunt three-word sentences while pouring their tortured souls from their stormy gazes. I spent last winter stuck in a remote cabin with my brother Gunnar, remember?"

Davis barked a laugh, though her comment twisted sharply in his chest. "My tortured soul is pouring from my gaze? What the heck does that even mean?"

She rounded and stalked back to him, stopping when their toes practically touched. His pulse hitched at her intensity.

"It means I can see the struggle you're having, can feel conflict fairly pulsing from you." She placed her palm over his heart, her words stripping his defenses and leaving him exposed. "You say I shouldn't trust you, which tells me you're waging a battle within that you can't see the end to. But I'm telling you right now, Davis Fields, no matter your past, no matter who you think you are, I know a decent, honorable, and caring man when I see one." She shrugged, a small smile lifting the corner of her mouth. "I grew up surrounded by examples of what a good man looks like, and you more than live up to them."

His throat ached with the power and conviction in her voice. He wanted her words to be true, to find his way back to who he always wanted to be. Maybe, with her help, the fight back wouldn't be so daunting.

He slipped one hand over hers, still pressed against his chest, then cupped the other around the back of her neck. Her lips parted slightly as she inhaled a shallow breath, then held it. Could she feel his heart hammering against his ribs? He slid his thumb across her pulse point in her neck and found it thumping like hummingbird wings.

He inched forward, her lemony exhale brushing his skin a second before he captured her satin lips with his. She sighed and leaned into him. Her hand twisted in his, her fingers threading through his own. She clung to him, wrapping her arms around his waist and pulling him closer. His hope thumped in his ears and soared higher than the clouds.

She pulled away a fraction of an inch, her lips brushing against his as she whispered, "Do you hear that?"

"All I hear is my pulse rushing in my ears." He kissed her again.

Her smile against his lips made him want to stay right there forever.

She pushed away from him. "It sounds like a helicopter."

He froze, all his senses zeroing in on what she heard. The *thump-thump* of a helicopter sounded in the distance. Sunny bounced on her toes, pulled him close, and pecked him on the mouth.

"Bjørn." She stepped away, excitement filling her face. "I *knew* my parents would send in the cavalry when

I didn't contact them." She pulled on Davis's hand. "Come on. We have to find an open space."

She rushed through the forest without waiting for a response. He took off after her, pulling his binoculars from the side pocket of his pack. If her brother Bjørn was there with his helicopter, searching for them, then Davis could get word to the authorities and take down the men responsible for Justin's death. Davis would make sure that the entire operation paid.

They broke through the forest and stumbled to a stop at the clearing riddled with blown down trees.

"Microburst." Sunny heaved out between breaths.

He'd heard of the tunnel of sinking air that could descend on an area during a thunderstorm. He'd just never seen the destruction it could create. There had to be at least a mile or two of trees jumbled like a giant game of pick-up sticks.

"Come on." Sunny rushed into the clearing, running along the length of the first downed tree, before jumping to the next.

Davis followed and quickly wished for a field of swampy muskeg. Picking his way through the mess of limbs and trees frustrated him with the exertion required. The helicopter's thumping grew louder.

"Sunny, wait."

He clambered up beside her and peered through the binoculars. A flash of light reflecting in the distance pulled his attention to the side of the machine. Something about the helicopter didn't seem right, but then again, Bjørn had gotten a new one since the last time Davis had talked to him. He adjusted the binoculars and handed them to her. Her chest heaved as she surveyed the helicopter for several seconds.

Her forehead creased and head shook. "That's not Bjørn."

She swallowed and looked at Davis. All the color drained from her face, leaving her bronzed skin chalky. If it wasn't Bjørn, then who else could be out in the wilderness this far?

"Maybe Dad contacted one of his friends at 40-Mile Air?" Her voice shook, not truly confident in the statement.

Davis wasn't waiting to find out. He scanned around them, angry that he'd let his guard down, and now they were stuck in a mess of logs. They wouldn't be able to get to the cover of the forest before they were spotted. He wanted a better look at the helicopter but needed to get that glimpse from cover before they showed themselves.

A stack of torn up trees bigger than the rest sat twenty feet away. Maybe they could hide underneath.

"Go." He pointed and pushed in the direction he indicated. "We need to hide."

She took off, jumping over tree trunks and roots like a gazelle, all while keeping as much debris between her and the helicopter's line of sight. He kept his gaze trained on the helicopter as he followed her. The longer he looked, the more convinced he was that it wasn't a local's helicopter used for guiding hunters. This bird was military-grade. He just wasn't sure if it was friend or foe.

When they made it to the bigger stack, relief flooded him at the pocket of space deep beneath the logs. He peeked over the top tree as Sunny climbed in, his anxiety ratcheting up as the helicopter veered its course toward them. Had they been spotted? It wasn't possible from that distance ... unless—he shoved the binoculars into his pack and pushed it ahead into the space beside Sunny.

"Do you have any emergency blankets?" His question came out sharp and quick as he dug through his pack.

"Yes." She didn't ask anything else, just got to work finding it.

"I've got this feeling—" He shook his head, not sure if he should trust his gut or if he was overreacting.

"Whatever it is, go with it." Sunny unfolded her emergency blanket, the silvery material crinkling in the small space. "I'm not about to second guess your intuition."

Her trust in him eased some of the doubt. Could he ever believe in himself with such confidence again? He shook off the question and focused on protecting Sunny.

"We need to stretch these out above us, but it can't be up against our bodies." He pulled his blanket open and poked a corner on a broken off tree branch.

"Okay." She didn't even ask why, just got to work.

His sister, Piper, would pepper him with questions. Not Sunny. She obviously understood the need to follow orders, probably because of her time on Denali and Everest. Could be from her family and their upbringing too. All the Rebels were more than equipped for trouble.

"The way the helicopter veered our way has me worried they might be equipped with heat-sensors." He shook his head, praying he was wrong. "These will help reflect our heat … hopefully. Probably."

"Wow. More than three words. I'm impressed." She speared her last corner onto a branch and turned to him with a strained smile.

He could barely make her out as the sunlight filtered

through the cracks, but the way the light reflected off their silver makeshift tent onto her determined expression blew him away. He motioned her to him.

"We need to stay beneath these." He patted the dirt beside him.

"So, more cuddling?" She wagged her eyebrows at him.

"Sunny." He chuckled, rolling his eyes.

How could she possibly be this calm, shining brightness even in this dark moment? She laid down beside him, curling into him. Her body trembled against his. So, she wasn't as unaffected as she let on.

"It's going to be okay." He pressed a kiss to her forehead. "I'm probably overreacting. As soon as they fly by, I'll sneak a peek and see if we can show ourselves."

"What if it's the bad guys?" She pulled back and glanced up at him.

"Then they'll fly right over and never know we're here."

"Okay." She closed her eyes and nodded, tucking herself back under his chin.

The helicopter drew closer, and for the first time in a long time, Davis prayed. Not for himself, but for Sunny's safety. The *thump-thump* drowned out all other sounds. Sunny shivered, and he pulled her tighter against him.

"Shh," he whispered against her hair, though he doubted she could hear him. "It's going to be ok—"

The rapid *pop-pop* from a M60E3 machine gun riddled the air, exploding in the downed trees just beyond them. Sunny shrieked, but quickly stifled it. Without hesitating, Davis rolled Sunny under him and shielded her with his body. Not that it would stop a bullet from piercing them both.

Bullets impacted on the other side of them. He took the chance of being seen and snagged his pack from where he'd pushed it just outside of their reflective protection. He'd never taken out the bulletproof plate lining the fabric against his backpack. It wasn't much protection, but it might slow a bullet down enough to not go through both of them.

"See anything on thermal?" A voice barely audible over the rotors shouted above them.

The pause lasted what seemed like forever. Sunny muttered prayers as her hands trembled where they clutched Davis's shirt. He focused on the noises above them. If he had to, he could use her gun to buy them some time and space. It wouldn't do much good against a machine gun, but he was a decent shot. If he could take out the shooter, then the tail rotor, the helicopter would go down.

"Yes, I'm sure ... movement over here." The voice shouted again, anger and frustration lacing his words.

Bullets peppered down. They exploded trees and debris, sending shards through the open space. Something hit his cheek, and he flinched, tucking his head and body more around Sunny to shield her. If the bullets hit any closer, their chances of living through the next minute plummeted. No one would ever know what happened to them or to Justin.

A bullet struck just to the left of him. Dirt kicked up, and Sunny trembled beneath him. The swatches of sunlight opened wider with each barrage. Soon, the shooter would be able to see the reflective material of the blanket. Davis was surprised the man hadn't already.

Davis had to act, do something to give them at least a chance at surviving. He stretched his hand to Sunny's pack, reaching in the concealed pouch for her gun. He would no longer cower like a groundhog, just waiting to get shot in the back.

Sunny's head snapped out from under his chin. Her wide eyes stared up at him as she shook her head. "Don't," she mouthed. His gaze bounced from one of her deep brown eyes to the other, probably pouring tortured soul all over her, but he didn't care. All that mattered was that he did everything he could to keep her safe.

"Stay here," he said, bending down and kissing her on the lips.

She wrapped her fingers into his shirt. "Davis, no."

He kissed her again, not wanting to leave. But if he didn't do something quick, they'd both be dead. He pried her fingers from the fabric and moved toward the opening.

Chapter Seventeen

IF THE SHOOTER in the helicopter didn't kill Davis, Sunny would. He placed his pack over her. The thing probably had some kind of armor or something, and, in that case, the dumb lug should keep it. Strap it to the front of him.

He made to crawl toward the opening, and the loneliness that had dragged her down the last year threatened to rip her apart from the inside and consume her. She pushed the pack off to the side, pressed her front to Davis's back, and wrapped her legs around his waist. His hands pried at her knees, but she hadn't spent years wrestling with her brothers and taking martial arts for nothing. She hooked her feet together, then snaked her arms around his and clasped her hands behind his head so his arms couldn't move.

Could he break out of the hold if he wanted? Probably. But she would clamp on for dear life, and him escaping would most likely hurt her. She was betting he wouldn't do that.

"Sunny." He grunted as he bent forward, trying to break her hold.

She locked her fingers tighter. Climbing mountains for a living made them strong. There was no way she would let go. She couldn't let these monsters kill someone else she cared about.

"You're not leaving me, so knock it off." Her muscles burned, begging for release.

Bullets exploded, further away than they'd been.

"Shh." She froze, making sure not to release him. "Are they leaving?"

The roar of the helicopter's rotors no longer thundered directly above them. More gunfire peppered down, but it wasn't anywhere near them. Had she and Davis really evaded them?

"Okay, you can let go now."

Cringing at the anger in Davis's voice, she inwardly sniffed. Let him be miffed. Being around growly people wasn't foreign to her. It was like family, though Davis's gruffness seemed deeper than her siblings. She smirked, then focused on the cranky man still trapped in her limbs.

"You done playing Rambo, saving the world on your own?" She squeezed her legs to emphasize her point.

He grunted.

"Is that superhero-speak for yes or no?"

"Yes." The word practically rumbled from him.

He relaxed against her, however she knew all about faking an opponent out. Her brother Tiikâan was the master of pretending to give up, only to pounce when she let her guard down. She adjusted her grip on her sweaty hands.

"Promise?"

Davis's sigh reached all the way to his toes. "Yes, I promise."

Back to three-word sentences? She didn't care, as long as he wasn't filled with bullet holes. Biting her bottom lip, she let her hands go. Davis spun so fast she didn't have time to react. His weight and heated gaze pinned her to the ground, thrumming excited adrenaline through her blood that burned the terror away.

"I don't want to save the world. Just you." His ragged voice had every one of her nerve endings on fire. "Only you."

His kiss was hard and desperate, filled with so much desire, yet tinged with undeniable fear. She wrapped her arms around his back, holding him as tightly to her as she could. Her own desperation and worry trembled through her fingers as she gripped the back of his shirt.

He trailed his lips along her jaw, his touch transforming from frantic to gentle, leaving her feeling cherished. His palm cupped her neck and his thumb rubbed her cheek. His shuddering breath against her ear raced a shiver of delight across her skin.

"I can't let them hurt you." His anguished tone and sucked inhale made stinging tears spring to her eyes.

She leaned her cheek against his and whispered, "And I'm not letting you go. Never again."

Kissing below his ear, she pressed a path through his tickling beard to his strong lips. No longer fueled by anger and fear, she lingered in the kiss, exploring the depth of her love in slow, vulnerable caresses.

Love?

Davis's fingers trembled as he trailed them along her cheek and through her hair, making that hole of loneliness in her heart close completely. Yeah. Her love may be new, like fireweed blossoms blooming low on the stalk, but the hope of it was there in her heart.

How could she prove to him she didn't need saving? That if they stuck together, they could conquer any obstacle or foe against them? Maybe telling him how much he meant to her would help him see that throwing himself in front of bullets would only break her.

She flinched at the thought and pulled back to look into his eyes. How could she have let herself fall in love so fast again? Hadn't she learned her lesson the last time? Her eyes stung, and she closed them, grasping for the fragments of strength being alone had cocooned her heart in. As much as she tried to pull her protective shield up, she couldn't.

Davis sighed and kissed one closed eye, then the other. "I'm sorry, Sunny."

He pressed his lips to her cheek, then her mouth. They tasted salty. Her forehead creased, and she opened her eyes to a blurry version of Davis.

"I don't need saving." She swallowed the sob that threatened to force its way out of her burning throat.

Davis closed his eyes and shook his head.

Maybe she hadn't learned from her past. Yet, everything in her screamed she had. That this man differed from the others—was someone she could trust with her hopes.

With her heart.

Chapter Eighteen

Sunny waited in the hole while Davis made sure the coast was clear. Carefully removing the silvery blankets from their protective positions, she cringed at the holes ripped through them. It truly was a miracle bullets hadn't riddled her and Davis, and they weren't bleeding out. Her hands shook as she folded the last blanket and shoved it into her pack.

Dirt rained down into the hole. She jumped and shrieked. Davis's low chuckle preceded his head filling the opening.

"You remain calm as a cucumber through gunfire, but scream now?" The sun behind his head shadowed his face, but she imagined he had that glorious one-sided smile he'd get sometimes when he watched her.

"Oh, shush." She shoved his pack out of the hole. "Give me a break. I'm coming down from DEFCON 5 in here. And, in case you didn't know, that was my first time being shot at with a machine gun from a helicopter."

He chuckled even more. "Baby, high alert is DEFCON 1."

The way he said baby, all low and slow, made the cool hole suddenly warm.

"Really?" She paused as she pushed her pack to him, hoping her blush would calm down, and tipped her head. "That's kind of backwards, isn't it? I mean, the scale is usually one to ten, with ten being the most. Why would they go backwards?"

"Because it's the military."

He waved his hand at her, like that was a good explanation. Then again, she'd heard all the stories her siblings and father told, so maybe it was the perfect explanation. She scrambled up the hole.

"Come on. Let's get out of here." He pulled her to her feet and softly pushed her hair out of her face, his whole soul pouring from his gaze in overdrive.

She could stand there forever and just soak in the care and, dare she think, love issuing from him.

"I'm glad that was your first experience with that. I'm going to do everything I can to make sure it doesn't happen again," he promised, and she believed him.

"I know." She smiled and kissed him, then took off toward the forest.

A young grizzly sprawled dead on the edge of the microburst. Dark blood saturated its coat in so many places, it almost looked black. Her head jerked back to Davis.

"They must've thought the bear was us at first and decided that was what they'd seen in their scan that originally drew them over here." He stepped up beside her and kissed her temple. "That bruin saved our lives."

"Poor thing." She skirted the carcass and beelined for the trees, tears stinging her eyes.

She hated that everywhere these people went, they left destruction and death. Would she and Davis even be able to make it to safety with the tech and weapons against them? If only they could get hold of help and turn the fight back on their enemies.

They walked in silence for what seemed like hours. She couldn't think of anything to say that wouldn't dissolve her into tears. Davis didn't mind the quiet. Probably spent hours not communicating when he was on missions with his special ops team.

The shade beneath the towering trees blocked the sun, which, ironically, she was thankful for. The day before, she would have cherished the warmth. She relished it, glad the rain had finally let up, and clear, blue skies stretched from horizon to horizon. However, the sun brought temperatures that had to be reaching in the nineties. That kind of heat for the Alaskan girl, more often on the frigid mountains than the tundra, left her roasting.

A clearing appeared through the low hanging birch branches. Hopefully, they'd find a creek they could get more water from. Her canteen hung light from her belt.

"Hold up." Davis commanded from behind her. "Let me take a look."

She heaved a sigh of relief and stretched her back as he snuck up to the edge of the clearing. When he continued to scan the surroundings, she rolled her eyes and dropped her pack to the ground. *This might take a while.*

She checked the InReach for a signal, again. But like the hundred times before, there still wasn't a signal, which made absolutely no sense. The InReach had worked at the North Pole. It should work.

Unhooking her water bottle, she took a sip. Until they found a water source, they'd have to be careful. She gritted her teeth as she capped the bottle. Could anything else go wrong?

She quickly took back that thought. Worry that even thinking such a thing would bring about more danger had her forcing thoughts of them finding a rushing creek that would not only give them sustaining water but lead them to civilization. She wasn't taking any chances the stray thought of doom and gloom would bring more trouble.

"We're clear." Davis turned to her, finally done with his reconnaissance or whatever he'd call it.

"Good. Let's see if we can find some water."

She walked up to him, ready to lead them on. Forcing a smile past her exhaustion, she winked at him when she drew close. As she passed, he grabbed her pack strap, pulled her to him, and kissed her so thoroughly, she had to lock her knees so they didn't buckle. When he stopped, her chest heaved as she tried to catch her breath.

"What was that for?" Her gaze glued to his lips, excitement unfurling as one side of his mouth tipped up into a cocky smile.

"I'm done pushing down the desire to kiss you sense-less." He moved his hand from her strap to cup her cheek, his thumb rubbing her bottom lip. "I've been doing that since I knocked you out and realized who you were." He snorted. "Shoot. I've been forcing myself to *not* kiss you since I pretended to be your boyfriend for your sister's wedding."

"Oh."

Oh? That's all she could come up with? Apparently senseless was the correct term.

Well, if he was going to kiss her willy-nilly, she'd embrace that logic as her own. Wrapping her hands around both his backpack straps, she rose to her toes and put all the love blooming in her heart into her kiss. He smiled against her mouth, sending lightning to strike chaotically in her stomach. His hands cupped her cheeks and tipped her head for a better angle.

Boy howdy.

Could this man kiss or what?

"Okay." He sucked in a breath and pulled away from her. "Maybe I need to change my original statement, because if we keep kissing whenever the desire hits, we aren't ever going to leave this spot."

"That's the truth." She bit her bottom lip and rocked back on her heels, letting his straps go.

"You can't do that."

Her forehead crinkled in confusion. "Do what?"

"Bite your lip like that." He groaned and took a step away from her. "You do that, and I want to dive back in."

She didn't stifle her smile, her teeth unconsciously pulling on her lip.

"Seriously. Go." He groaned again and pushed her into the clearing.

Her laugh floated up her chest and out. Joy saturated her cells, making her feel alive for the first time in months. Here she was, running for her life from gun-wielding maniacs, and yet she was happy. She'd take it, cherishing the feeling for as long as she could.

"Wonder what used to be out here?" Davis's question jerked her back from her woolgathering.

She snickered at the word and scanned their surroundings. A long, skinny clearing edged a cliff that tapered down to a meadow. The descent where they'd emerged was too steep and high to climb down, so they'd work their way to the meadow. The tall willows told her whoever had chopped the trees down had done so several years, if not decades, before.

"Maybe it was an old mine." She picked a game trail to follow through the thick, spindly willows. "I bet they had cleared it for exploratory purposes. It doesn't seem wide enough and there aren't any tailings for actual mining. Hopefully, this trail the animals left will lead us to water. I'm getting low."

"Me too."

She stepped over a crack in the earth. With earthquakes and thawing permafrost, a lot of the Alaskan ground constantly shifted. Made maintaining roads and houses a struggle.

"Might even find an old cabin or something we can camp in for the night," Davis said from right behind her.

"That'd be nice." She glanced at her watch, surprised it was already late in the evening.

The long summer days with endless light really messed with one's sense of time. No wonder her feet weighed twenty pounds each. If they didn't find a place to hole up soon, she might just collapse.

She jumped down from another crack, Davis's thump chasing hers. The ground shifted beneath her feet. She stumbled backward, bumping into Davis, embarrassed that she was so tired she couldn't even walk straight.

Chuckling, she turned to him. "Thanks for catch—"

The earth disappeared from under them. Her chuckle caught in her throat in a silent scream. She knocked her head against the ground as she fell. Stars exploded in front of her eyes before everything went black.

Chapter Nineteen

NINE MONTHS Earlier

Day 1: Fake Relationship with a Real-Life Hero

Sunny glanced around the bustling Louisville Muhammad Ali International Airport but felt little of the excitement places of travel usually gave her. Her eyes skimmed unfocused over faces, not seeing the details she once cherished. No harried family twisted her heart with empathy. No cocky teen made her laugh as he puffed up like a rooster when he noticed her. She couldn't even muster the energy to search for her favorite sight. In every airport, she could always find at least one older couple that doted on each other, taking care of one another in little ways that always filled her heart with warmth and longing.

Surely, Jed hadn't stolen her joy of watching people along with her money.

"I'm glad both you and Davis were able to get here before the wedding. It'll give Carter time to get comfortable around you two." Her sister Lena shook Sunny out of her dreary, downward spiral. "You sure you're up for this? Carter can be a handful."

Lena's doubt as she inspected Sunny's face twisted like a sharp knife in the chest. In truth, the pitying looks she caught from her family and friends had just as much to do with her numbness as having the man she had started entertaining ideas of marriage with stealing her livelihood. Did that one mistake of trusting the wrong person negate everything else she'd done in life?

Sunny rolled her eyes in mock exasperation. "Carter loves me. He'll be fine. Will you?"

Lena bit her bottom lip in uncertainty, her alert gaze searching for a threat in the crowd. "Honestly? I don't know. Since the kidnapping, he hasn't been the same." She snorted a self-deprecating laugh. "None of us have. Maybe we shouldn't leave him."

When Carter had been kidnapped, Lena almost lost everything she loved for the second time in her life. Sunny couldn't imagine all they went through. But she didn't want Lena to cancel her honeymoon out of fear.

"Hey. He'll be fine. You've got the best security team out there, *and* you're bringing in this Davis guy under-cover, which I have to say I'm excited about. Pretending to be in love with one of your sexy military friends won't be a hardship on me." Sunny bumped her shoulder against Lena's. "The chances of anyone getting past all that is practically zero. Plus, I'm like the coolest aunt ever. Carter will be having so much fun, he'll forget you're even gone."

"Thanks, I think." Lena scowled. "Listen, about Davis."

She paused, drawing Sunny's attention. Her sister

fidgeted, which Lena never did. Just what about this guy had Lena hemming and hawing?

When she didn't continue, Sunny prompted her. "Yeah?"

"He'd kill me if he knew I told you this, so don't say a word to him." Lena gave Sunny a pointed look.

"I won't. Scouts honor." She held her fingers up in salute.

"He's having a hard time adjusting to civilian life. Maybe it's more…"

When Lena paused, Sunny couldn't keep the question in. "More?"

"Ugh. Maybe something happened before he got out that's bothering him. I don't really know." Lena huffed out a sigh. "He doesn't really talk to anyone about it. Just don't take it personal if he's standoffish."

"So, you've put me in a fake relationship with a grump?" Sunny lifted her hands in exasperation, though a sense of solidarity fluttered in her chest. "How's this supposed to work exactly then?"

"I don't know. I guess … just … grrr." Lena growled and crossed her arms. "Remember how angry I was after Ethan died?"

"Yeah." Sunny swallowed. Had Davis gone through something as horrible as Lena had not being able to save her fiancé?

"Just … don't be disappointed if Davis doesn't play his part well." Lena whispered the last.

Sunny's heart clenched in her chest. Was heartache all that was left in the world? She glanced around the busy luggage area, noticing for the first time all the frustrated, angry, and weary faces. She closed her eyes and shook her head. She didn't want to be that bitter person. Didn't want to only see the bad in others.

Maybe this fake relationship was exactly what she needed to get out of her funk. Maybe it could be the break she needed to just forget reality and pretend like her life hadn't been swept away like an avalanche leaving her buried in distrust and failure.

"Okay. Here we go." Lena's anxious words snapped Sunny's gaze to the escalator.

A man with a large pack slung over his shoulders stepped onto the escalator. His short dark, brown hair and rigid posture as he scanned the area below him screamed military. He was ridiculously handsome and incredibly built, with his t-shirt stretching over muscles she could see even from this far away. When his scan stopped on her and Lena and he tipped his head in acknowledgement, Sunny snapped her mouth shut.

"That superior specimen of man is my fake boyfriend?" She hit her sister with the back of her hand as she gaped at Davis.

"Yep."

"Oh, man. This is going to be a rough three weeks."

Sunny couldn't stifle her smile as her mood lifted. A soft squeal behind her had her turning just in time to see a young couple embrace. An idea popped in her head, one she'd always fantasized about but had never thought would actually happen. But would she have the courage to go through with it?

She looked back at Davis just stepping off the escalator. She bit her bottom lip, then shrugged. What was the point of having a fake relationship if you couldn't have fun with it? Besides, if any baddies Lena was paranoid about were watching, it was Sunny's duty to make this relationship believable.

"Here. Hold my purse." She whacked her purse into Lena's gut.

"Wait. Where are you going?" Lena fumbled with the purse.

Sunny turned back to her sister, giving a devious lift of her eyebrow. "Why, I'm going to greet my boyfriend I've missed desperately."

She winked then pushed through the crowd.

"Sunny! Don't do anything embarrassing," Lena said from behind Sunny

"When have I ever done that?"

"Constantly when we were growing up."

"I can't help it that I'm spontaneous and fun and you're not." She threw over her shoulder before waving her hand in the air. "Davis!"

Her shout drew the gazes of several around her. She broadened her smile as she saw Davis's head snap her direction. He looked left and right, his forehead furrowed in confusion, before focusing back on her.

"Davis!" She yelled again, causing an older man to chuckle in front of her.

"Young love." He laughed.

"Remember when we were like that, dear?" The old man's wife asked.

Sunny beamed a full-toothed smile at the couple and shrugged. "Sorry."

"Go get him, sweetie, and don't let go." The woman waved Sunny on.

A twinge of regret soured the moment. If only she was rushing toward the love of her life and not just pretending. She shook off the feeling and focused on the fun of doing something so completely wild and carefree.

When the crowd cleared for her like the parting of the Red Sea, she sprinted toward Davis. His stoic face was even more handsome the closer she got. His dark brown eyes widened in shock a moment before she threw herself at him.

His duffle hit the ground with a thump, and he caught her against himself, which was good since she hadn't considered what would happen if he didn't. She wrapped her arms and legs around him like she'd seen in countless videos and kissed him. He froze, his fingers tightening around her waist.

The shock must have worn off, because his arms banded around her like he would carry her forever and never let go. His kiss held the same sense of desperation she had in her heart and tried to hide from everyone else. When she slowed the kiss and pulled back slightly, surprise still shone from his eyes.

"Hi. I'm Sunny," she whispered as she tried to catch her breath.

His lips hitched up on one side, tempting her to kiss them again. "Nice to meet you, Sunny."

"You two done?" Lena broke in, exasperation so thick in her voice Sunny almost started kissing Davis again just to annoy her sister more.

She did get another peck in before unwrapping her legs from his waist. He reached down with one hand to snag his duffle, saying a terse greeting to Lena. After Lena turned toward the entrance, Davis glanced hesitantly at Sunny before sliding his arm around her waist and pulling her next to him. Her pulse jumped in her throat. She wasn't sure how fake relationships worked, exactly, but so far, this one beat any real relationship she'd had to date.

Davis's stomach flew into his throat as he fell. He clawed at the dirt walls, trying to slow down his descent. Sunny flopped into him, and he wrapped his arms around her limp body to protect her as they fell. The slam into the ground shot red-hot pain through his shoulder and ripped the air from his lungs.

He couldn't breathe. Letting Sunny roll off of him to the ground, he sat up and jerked off his pack, taking deep breaths through his mouth and pushing his stomach out to get his diaphragm to calm down. He kept his hand wrapped around Sunny's strap, just in case the earth took them on another wild ride.

When his diaphragm stopped spasming, he reached out with his other hand to pull Sunny to him. Sharp pain rushed down his arm, turning his fingers numb. He groaned and gritted his teeth against the agony. Hopefully, his shoulder wasn't all the way out of socket.

Ignoring his injury, he dragged Sunny to him with his good arm. He checked her vitals, tears blurring his already limited vision. He couldn't lose her.

Her strong pulse and even breathing released all the tension bundled in his muscles. He bent over her, a tortured sob rending from within. He tried to shut down the cascade of emotions slamming through him, but he'd lost his vise on them. All the pain, guilt, fear, and grief of the last few years tumbled over him in crushing waves. He'd gotten his team killed with his gullibility, had pushed away anyone who ever cared about him, been paranoid and unable to trust to the point of panic, and, even now, in the middle of the Alaskan wilderness with no one around, he'd failed.

The one person who had tempted him from his darkness lay crumpled and unconscious in some godforsaken pit. He should've noticed the unstable ground. If he'd been alert and led instead of being mesmerized by the sway in Sunny's dark ponytail, remembering the silky feel of it between his fingers, he would have taken them around the area.

"Get it together, soldier," he mumbled to himself.

This blubbering wasn't helping them any. Drawing on his years of training, he sucked in air through his teeth to calm himself down. He stopped the sobs, but he couldn't control the way his body trembled. An assessment needed to be made so they could figure out what to do next.

He straightened and stared at Sunny cradled against him, though the light barely illuminated her. He peered up, and his throat dried at the chasm above them. The gap had to be at least fifty feet deep. There was no way they should've survived that fall.

Swallowing, he glanced down at Sunny's still form. She might be breathing, but if she didn't wake up, if she'd hit her head hard enough, they wouldn't survive. His fingers trembled as he skimmed them across her cheek and into her hair. A large, sticky bump already formed by her temple.

"Wake up, Sunny." His voice broke, but he didn't care that his weakness showed. "I need that beautiful brain of yours to help me figure out how to get out of this mess."

His tears dropped onto her skin, reflecting in the

small amount of light filtering to their spot. He sniffed and wiped them off her cheek, bile rising as blood smeared where he touched. He cleaned his fingers on his shirt, but try as he might, he couldn't get the blood off her face. Cringing as his shoulder protested his movement, he unbuckled her pack and pulled it off her. The pain in his shoulder was nothing compared to the anguish in his heart.

"Come on, Firefly. Open those dark brown eyes of yours." He shook her, then pulled her up to his chest and rocked her. "I need to see them. Need you."

"Davis?" While her whisper was barely audible, it echoed through his body.

He let her down so he cradled her in his good arm and could make her out in the waning light. He'd never felt such immense relief, not even in all his years in the military. Nor had he ever seen anything more beautiful than her looking up at him. She lifted her hand and cupped his cheek in her palm. He squeezed his eyes closed and pressed her hand between his face and palm.

"Why do you call me that?" Her question snapped his eyes open, and he stared at her in confusion.

"What?"

"Why do you call me Firefly?" She threaded her fingers through his and brought their joined hands to rest against her chest with a sigh. "I've always wondered."

Could he tell her? Could he let down the last of his guards? He was blubbering like a baby. Couldn't get any more vulnerable than that. Apparently, he already speared her with his feelings when he looked at her. He scrunched his forehead and shook his head. Feelings weren't right. More like soul-stretching, heart-pounding love.

"No?" Her voice cracked, and she covered it with a laugh. "You don't want to tell me?"

Might as well follow up all that gaze-oozing he was doing with words.

"Do you remember when we first met?" He rubbed his thumb across her fingers, watching the motion instead of her reaction.

"Are you kidding? That was one of the most memorable moments of my life." She laughed, then winced. "Not only did I get the handsomest fake boyfriend ever, but I got to embarrass my sister and have an iconic airport kissing scene of my own."

Davis shook his head, a smile playing at his lips. "I wasn't too thrilled about going to Lena's wedding and having to pretend to be your boyfriend." Sunny gasped, and he quickly added. "It had nothing to do with you. I just was already so tired. Tired of being on guard all the time. Tired of pretending, of constantly looking over my shoulder, waiting for an attack. More than anything, I was exhausted with myself, with my edginess and anger. The last thing I wanted was to be stuck babysitting while playing a role. Babysitting was hard enough.

"So, my mood coming off that plane wasn't the best, even though I'd talked myself in circles, determined not to ruin Lena's wedding. She deserves happiness after everything she's been through. I was nervous about the whole fake boyfriend thing." He chuckled, trying to make light of everything, but it fell flat. "I mean, I couldn't even pretend to be happy around my family. How was I going to pull off being an enamored boyfriend? The last thing I expected when I walked off that escalator was for you to run up to me and jump into my arms like I was someone worth getting excited over."

"I couldn't believe you caught me." She sighed.

"I couldn't believe you trusted me to." He hitched one side of his mouth up. "When you started kissing me, I was so shocked, I almost dropped you."

"You recovered quickly, if I remember right."

"Yeah. That's because you burned the shock and unease away, leaving only this brightness I wanted to cling to."

He could barely make out her smile. She pulled his hand to her lips and kissed his knuckles. He couldn't hide his body's flinch of pain the motion caused.

"You're hurt." Sunny sat up, placing her hand to her head. "Whoa."

"Hey, take it easy." He lifted his uninjured arm and pushed her sticky hair away from her face. "You've got a good wound to your head. I need to check it more closely."

She waved him off. "I've got a hard skull. It'll hold." She skimmed her hands over his torso and arms. "Where are you hurt?"

"My shoulder." He tipped his head to the right. "It acts up occasionally. It's not all the way out of socket, but it's close."

"Okay."

She dug through her pack, pulled out a glow stick, and snapped it to mix the chemicals. The bright green light made the blood smeared across her cheek and wetting her hair more ghastly. Dread coiled in his gut.

He was going to watch her die.

Could feel it in his bones.

He tore his gaze from her and scanned their

surroundings. Man-made walls reached about seven feet from the ground. A tunnel went off beyond the reach of the light. Had they fallen into a mineshaft? That didn't seem right, but he couldn't explain the deep cavern any other way.

"All righty. Let's take a look at your arm." Her false cheer dragged his gaze back to her.

She skimmed her fingers up his arm and pushed on the shoulder. The dull ache spiked to sharp pain. He hissed, squeezing his eyes closed so he wouldn't pull away.

"You're right. It's not out all the way." When she finished her examination, she gently massaged up his neck. "This has happened before?"

"Yeah."

"How did you fix it?"

"Shotgun."

Her guffaw cut short. "What?"

"If I hold the butt of the gun wrong against my shoulder, the recoil will knock it back into place." He shrugged, immediately regretting the motion.

"Well, we don't have one of those."

"I've had buddies punch it back into place when it happened in the field."

She shook her head. "I throw a mean punch, but I don't know …"

"Hey, it's okay. We can figure it out later."

"No, no. Let's try." She shifted, then shook her head. "We'll have to stand. I can't get enough momentum on the ground."

This was why he loved her. Well, one reason. She just accepted each challenge head on, confident they could figure it out. He groaned as he stood, feeling every bruise from the fall now that the adrenaline was gone.

"So … Firefly?" Sunny raised her eyebrow at him before squaring up to his shoulder in a boxer's stance.

"Why did you greet me the way you did at the airport?" He wasn't sure why the question came out, but he needed to know.

"I'd been feeling lost. Was so sick of everyone asking if I was okay. I just wanted to forget how everything had been stolen from me. Forget how everyone looked at me with pity or, worse, caution, like I couldn't handle adult situations, which, considering how completely naïve I'd been, I totally understand the lack of confidence in my decisions." Her voice broke, and she rolled her shoulders. "Then, you came down that escalator with your gorgeous self, shifting like you were nervous, and I wanted to let the pretend be as real as possible, to escape, even if it was just for a few weeks." Her hands dropped and shoulders slumped. "Pretty pathetic."

"Being with you that week leading up to the wedding, then the two weeks after babysitting Carter while Lena and Marshall were on their honeymoon, was the first time I'd felt hope since my team got ambushed. You flashed light and joy in my darkness, making me think that if I could just catch you, I might keep that happiness your presence lit inside me." He closed his eyes, remembering how reality had crashed in. "But I knew I had to let you go, that I'd just suffocate you. Kill off your light like I did everything else good in my life."

Her fist slammed into his shoulder. He yelled at the shock and pain as the ball of his shoulder popped back into place. His knees collapsed, and he dropped to the dirt, stopping himself from completely crumpling to the ground with his good hand.

She was in front of him before he could catch his breath. Her small, strong hands clasped his cheeks and lifted his head. She pressed her lips to his. They were moist and tasted salty. He ran his thumb along her skin, wiping tears from where they streamed. She pulled away just enough to talk, her lips brushing against his as she did.

"You don't stifle me, Davis Fields. With you, I shine brighter than I ever have. With you, I finally feel whole, like I can be exactly who I'm meant to be. No pretending. No falsehoods." She kissed him, pushing out the darkness saturating his soul. "With you, I'm finally free."

He buried his face into the crook of her neck and wrapped her tight against him. Her skin smelled of musty dirt, metallic blood, and faint lemons. His shoulders shook as elation and heartbreak collided within. How could life be so harsh to finally have him find healing and hope when their survival was doomed?

Chapter Twenty

Sunny sat cross-legged on the ground and pulled her portable camp stove out of her pack while Davis paced down the tunnel shooting off their landing spot … again. They'd already searched the space and found nothing but a broken lantern and a jumble of boulders completely blocking the exit. She glanced up at the hole they'd fallen through. Not much could be seen except the soft yellowish blue sky left from the midnight sun through the small opening. At least it wasn't raining.

Focusing back on the task at hand, she unwrapped one of her emergency fuel packets of twigs and lint, just enough to heat one small pot of water. She only had three more packets, so if they didn't get out soon, they'd be eating her freeze-dried meals crunchy. Grabbing her canteen, she cringed as she remembered their supply of water. They might run out of it before they ran out of food.

She shook her head and focused on facts. There wasn't any use spiraling down the We're-Going-To-Die

Trail. That wouldn't help the situation and would lead to stupid decisions.

Davis's frustration roared from the tunnel, followed by something smashing against the wall. She hated that he thought this was his fault, like his superhuman military training should have warned him the earth was unstable. They'd been walking over land exactly like the ground above all day without it opening up like some horror movie to swallow them whole. A shiver slid down her spine like a seal on ice.

"Stop it, you ninny," she whispered to herself.

She'd been in similar situations while climbing. Granted, her climbing group had been equipped with homing beacons and the hope of rescue, but that didn't change the facts. If she wanted to survive this, they needed to economize their actions and their supplies. She closed her eyes to the headache pounding behind them and rubbed her fingers over her forehead.

"Davis." She barely spoke above a whisper.

She needed his help to figure out their situation. Her head hurt too much to do it on her own. Plus, his stomping and grunting only increased her dread. When he didn't come, she tried a little louder.

"Davis." Her voice cracked, and his footsteps rushed toward her.

She warmed at the thrill he'd hurry to her side with just her saying his name. The worried crease in his forehead and panicked look in his eyes as he emerged from the tunnel chilled the blush. This man held so much grief and responsibility on his shoulders. She didn't want to add any more, yet they had to figure out their supplies and a rationing schedule.

She forced a smile to ease him. "I need your help organizing things. My brain's a little too tired to think it through."

"Well, that's easy." He pushed his hand through his hair, then motioned to the packs. "You get it all."

She rolled her eyes. "Davis."

"I'm serious." He crossed his arms over his chest.

"I'm just as stubborn." She lifted her eyebrow to him.

"Yeah, but I've had training in going without."

"Just drop it, Fields." She shook her head, winced, then pulled more gear from her pack. "I'm dividing our supplies, whether or not you help. If you don't use your half, fine. It'll be waiting for the next poor soul that falls down here."

Infuriating man and his chivalrousness. Yanking out her phone, she turned it on, ignoring the huffing and heated glare hitting her from above. He kept forgetting, thanks to her brothers, she was impervious to cranky men. What they needed was music, something to relax them, maybe dispel the despair, even for a moment.

When the phone powered up, she tapped on her favorite playlist. The peppy intro for Woody Herman's "Woodchopper's Ball" filled the cavern, instantly lifting her spirit. She closed her eyes, letting the music wash over her. Her shoulders swayed and knee bounced to the happy beat.

She set the phone aside, now ready to tackle the harrowing job of rationing. Davis growled and mumbled something under his breath. Then he plopped down next to her and jerked his bag to him.

"What was that, dear?" She leaned her face toward him and batted her eyelids.

"Oh, nothing. I'm agreeing with you." His false cheer had her eyes slitting.

"Really. About what?"

"About you being hardheaded."

She laughed, then cut it short, placing her hand on her head. "Oh, don't make me laugh."

"I should check you again." Davis's playful tone fled with the mention of her injury, and she mentally chided herself for reminding him of it.

"I'm fine. Really. Just a nasty headache is all." She leaned closer before adding, "Now, my lips, on the other hand, might need examining. They're cold."

He froze, his exasperation shifting to desire and sending tendrils of heat rushing along her nerves. He lifted his hand, curled his fingers around her chin, and ran his thumb over her lips. Though he didn't move closer, the space between them filled until it was hard to breathe.

"You're right," he whispered, never taking his eyes off her mouth. "They *are* chilled."

He brushed them again but didn't close the distance separating them. Oh, what a dangerous game she'd started. One she didn't think she could win, not with the way she wanted to grab his shirt, yank him to her, and kiss the living daylights out of him. She remembered what he'd said earlier in the forest.

"Is there anything we can do to warm them?" She pulled her bottom lip between her teeth and bit down.

He erased the space between them faster than she could take a breath. Smiling against his lips, she kissed him without inhibition, letting her love and their undeniable connection lift her spirits even higher. If she was going to be trapped in a mineshaft, she couldn't imagine a better person to be stuck with. Or a better way to pass the time.

He lingered through the touch, her temperature rising with each tender moment. His love made her feel powerful and precious at the same time. He said she brightened his darkness, but he incinerated all her own loneliness and doubt in a burning wildfire.

How much time had passed when he slowed the kiss? Did it matter? She held his cheeks, spearing her fingers through his beard he'd grown since the wedding the fall before, and pressed another fervent kiss before pulling away.

His cocky smile lifted one side of his mouth, tempting her to go back for seconds. Or would that be thirds? Who cared? She wanted more.

He chuckled low, the elusive sound rolling in her stomach, and rubbed his thumb across her lips again. "There. All warmed."

"For now." She kissed his thumb, then turned back to the supplies. "They might get cold later, though."

"And I will be more than happy to remedy that problem." He nuzzled her neck, and she squealed at the way his beard tickled.

"Geesh. I'm trying to focus here." She bumped him with her shoulder.

"Right." He squeezed her in a tight hug before letting her go with a sigh. "Back to seeing how long we have before we die."

She rolled her eyes, determined not to let him drag her down. She lined her food out, adding the few supplies he'd had in his tent as he handed it to her. Five minutes later, their evaluation calculated to two more days of water if they consumed the bare minimum. Their food that didn't need rehydrated could last them five days, so at least they wouldn't starve first.

Davis's dark cloud of despair settled back over his countenance and radiated off him to her. The melancholy trumpets of Otis Redding's "Try a Little Tenderness" played on her phone, and Otis's soulful voice crooned about weariness that matched Davis's mood more than hers. Maybe the singer's advice would work on men too. She stood and extended her hand to Davis.

"Dance with me?"

He tore his gaze from the paltry supplies and looked at the phone like he just realized it was playing music. His expression when he finally looked up at her was so full of longing and sorrow her throat ached like she'd swallowed sharp ice. He took her hand and slowly stood, wrapping their clasped hands behind her back. As he moved up her, he swayed to the music, his forehead trailing up the center of her body until he tucked his head against hers.

She took her free hand and spread it across his slumped shoulders. Pressing her fingers into his muscle, she prayed he'd just release the weight he carried there and trust that the two of them together could figure a way out. As the music built, he squeezed her fingers still clutched in his behind her back and rolled her into a languid dip. He kissed the spot on the base of her neck where her collarbones met and, just as slowly, pulled her back up.

Next, he slid his other hand up her arm, grabbed her fingers, and twisted their arms over her head so she was tucked into his side. He rested his forehead to hers and swayed side to side for a couple of beats before he spun her back around.

She'd discovered he could dance at Lena's reception, but that had been different, more robotic, even though he'd spun her dizzily around the dance floor. The way he clung to her now, each move keeping her close, even through the complicated arm motions and spins, opened her heart to more fully let him in. He cherished her in a way no one had ever done before. Needed her as much as she needed him.

The song ended, changing over to Etta James's hopeful song, "At Last." He placed her arms on his shoulders and spread his hands up her back, pulling her flush against him. His fingers trailed up her spine, across her shoulders, and along her arm.

"'… a dream that I can call my own,'" he added his smooth baritone to Etta's, and Sunny gasped in pleasure.

"You know the words?" She whispered the question against his cheek.

"This amazing person introduced me to a great music era, and now I'm hooked." He did another rolling dip and murmured in her ear when he locked her to him. "Now, no more talking. I'm singing to my girl."

He crooned the rest of the song, kissing her neck, her lips, her cheeks as he bared his soul to her. She knew music held emotion. That's why she loved the oldies. She just never knew it could splay her open and lay everything bare. The song ended and a jaunty swing came on, but Davis kept the pace slow.

"I love you, Sunny." He gazed down at her in the pale green light the glow stick cast.

"I love you too," she whispered around the boulders clogging her throat.

His lips twitched into a smile before he pressed a soft kiss to hers. Then he tucked her against his chest and swayed. He never picked up the pace, but she didn't care. He pinned her right where she wanted to be.

Chapter Twenty-One

THE WAY Sunny stared up at the hole above them made Davis's meager breakfast curdle in his stomach. Her wheels spun, and he had a feeling he wouldn't like what she stopped on. Maybe if he could distract her, he could come up with his own plan for escape.

"Did your camera charge?" That was one thing to guarantee a shift in her attention.

She turned her gaze to him, her forehead scrunching in an adorable look of confusion before clearing in recognition. Just what had she been calculating that had her that deep in thought? As she dug through her pack, Davis peered up at the sky.

"Please, please, please." She chanted while she unplugged it from the travel battery charger and pressed the power button.

The little screen flashed, and he suddenly wished it hadn't charged. Whatever her camera had caught, he didn't want to watch it. Didn't want her to watch it. They'd been so focused on escaping and surviving, it had been easy to forget what had started their flight of horror.

"Yes." Her sharp exclamation made him flinch.

He hid it by shifting to sit next to her. The camera trembled in her hands as she cued up the last video.

"The last video is two hours long. I had just swapped a new battery not thirty minutes before I reached your camp." She sighed and looked at him, relief streaming from her gaze. "There has to be evidence on here that can be used, right?"

"I don't know." He swallowed, hoping what he said next worked. "Does it matter right now? Will it help our situation any?"

"No, but I have to know. It probably doesn't make sense, but I have to know at least one thing is in our favor." She ran her finger over the screen.

"Do you really want to witness what happened again? Right now?" He certainly didn't.

"No." She shook her head, adding emphasis to her statement and confusing him.

"Then why not wait?"

"Because … because I don't want to be the person who shies away from the difficult." She sniffed and speared him with a fiery look of stubbornness. "I have to watch, have to know there is hope that the truth of Justin's murder will be known. If I know that, I'll push that much harder, risk that much more. His death can't go unpunished. It can't."

"I get that."

She pressed play, then fast forwarded through the first bit. When the equipment at the mine site came into view, his pulse picked up like it was on 4x speed too. The footage started down the trail he'd walked a hundred times or more, and she switched the playback to normal speed. He held his breath.

"I can't wait to see the shocked look on his face when he sees me just walk out of the woods." Sunny's excited voice sounded from the camera's speaker.

She sucked in a breath beside Davis, her hand shaking as she covered her mouth. He scooted so his hip pressed to hers, wrapped one arm behind her back, and cradled her hand holding the camera with his other. She leaned against him, making the next few moments easier to bear.

A door slammed in the footage. The willows rushed past and opened into the camp's clearing, with Justin standing, alive and whole. Gun shots, then Sunny's scream on the video filled the cavern, chasing skittering chills across his skin. He never should've let her watch this.

"Did you hear that?" She cued the footage back.

"I never want to hear that again."

"No, listen." She pressed play and tipped her head.

Tires splashed.

A door slammed.

Voices.

She stopped it right before Justin's murder and cued it back again. This time she turned the volume up all the way, lifted the speaker right next to their heads, and cupped her hands around the camera to amplify the sound. Davis stared into her eyes as he concentrated on the voices.

"Zhang says you're causing too much trouble." He'd recognize the shooter's partner's cold voice anywhere.

"Sorry, man, we can't have you snooping, not when

we're this close to launching." The shooter spoke in a casual, friendly tone.

Sunny stopped the video and lowered the camera. "Launching what?"

"No clue. The mine, maybe?" Davis took the camera from her, turned it off, and tucked it in her case.

"Yeah, maybe." She shook her head, then stared up at the hole like it might hold the answer. "But why the comment about snooping? I mean, an exploratory mining company has all kinds of regulations and inspections, so it'd be hard to hide anything worth snooping over."

"Not necessarily." Memories of the mission he'd lost his team on rose like a submarine surfacing too fast. "There are lots of ways to hide nefarious actions."

"What do you mean?" She placed a hand on his, stilling his trembling fingers picking at nothing on his jeans.

He couldn't explain without telling her what had happened. Dread swirled like cold, loose mud in his core. Would he lose her trust when she realized he was responsible for his team members' deaths?

"When we were last stationed in the Middle East, we protected an area that was relatively peaceful. We didn't even know why we were there. Figured the military had us wasting time, chasing goats again." All the grief and pain balled in his throat. He tried to clear it free. "There was this young twelve-year-old boy, Faris Majid, who would come around almost every day. Well, there were a lot of kids, but he stuck out."

Davis could still picture the boy's face clearly, how intelligence and wonder always shone there. The other kids would get excited about the candies and trinkets.

Faris never cared about that. He was more interested in learning, specifically English. When he'd asked Davis to tutor him so he could go to university, Davis reveled in the opportunity. Finally, instead of violence, he'd sow hope.

"His dad ran a learning institute for training young adults job skills. At least, that's what they claimed." Davis squeezed his eyes shut. "We didn't realize the truth until Faris lured us in with a panicked plea for help from attackers. My team and another unit rushed from the base, only to be ambushed once we entered the institute."

"What happened?" Her hand slid along his shoulder, and he opened his eyes.

"We'd been lied to, by Faris and the CIA." He shook his head with a snort. "The boy was part of an extremist group infiltrating the area. That's why we'd been sent there. Only the CIA didn't think we needed to be privy to that intel. I should've known something was up. I'd been too lax, too trusting, and eager to see peace in all that violence. My foolishness cost so many lives."

"Davis—"

"No, Sunny, don't say it wasn't my fault." He brushed her hand off his shoulder and stood. "In all the times we'd gone to that institute, we never saw what it really was. It was so obvious afterward, but before? We believed the lies spun to us."

"Well, whatever is going on at this so-called mine needs to be exposed." She stood and peered up the shaft, dropping the subject of his guilt like she knew he needed to move off the topic. "Speaking of exploratory mining, I think that's what this was. See how there's two half-circles on either side of the gap?"

He followed her pointed finger to the opening. Sure enough. Faint perfect lines could be seen among the jagged.

"I think whoever did this was drilling to test the soil." She shrugged. "I'm not sure why they tunneled in from the cliff side instead of just bulldozing."

"Maybe they wanted to make sure something was worth hauling the big equipment all the way up here for."

"That makes sense." She stared back up at the opening. "I'm going to climb up."

After all he'd been through, he never thought fear would threaten to kill him.

"Sunny—"

"I've trained for this exact situation—"

"You've trained for falling down mine shafts?" He knew he was being contrary, but he couldn't help the gruff tone.

"No, but I trained for free climbing up ice walls inside crevasses." She trailed her finger along the seam above them. "Except for that vein of black sand in the middle, this fault runs along solid bedrock. The surface is jagged, not smooth, so there should be plenty of hand and footholds."

"Sunny, this isn't Denali where you are equipped with ice hooks and boot crampons."

"Lucky for us, I packed my trusty rope and a bag of cams." She winked at him and bent to her gear. "And with your injured shoulder, I get to play hero this time."

"I don't like it." Fear snaked and bit up his throat.

"I know." She straightened and stepped up so they were toe to toe. "But we don't have any other option."

"You sure?"

Without a doubt, her plan would work. Free climbing wasn't a walk in the park though, especially not with a head injury. But out of the two of them, she was the better climber.

"Well, we don't have time to find it." She kissed him gently, then went back to inspecting her climbing gear.

He peered up at the fissure, his head spinning with their only solution. Yep, her stubbornness would give him ulcers. Her steady fingers inspected the cams throughly, her face beautiful in its intense concentration. Sighing, he kneeled to help her. If he couldn't back her up with this, then any hope of a relationship was doomed.

Chapter Twenty-Two

Taking a deep breath, Sunny leaned back against the harness, testing the cam she'd just set into the rock. When it held, she relaxed and shook out her arms, letting the rope hold her. She inspected the crack in the wall she'd found halfway up the fissure. The line intersected an overhang that jutted out into the opening.

Huffing out a frustrated breath, she gnawed on her bottom lip. From the base, the ledge hadn't appeared so deep. Now that she could clearly see it, the realization that she should've picked a different route five feet to her left had her quivering. Nerves sent a rivulet of icy sweat on a path down her already chilled back.

"It's no big deal." She tore her gaze from the obstacle above as her head spun, and she checked her harness. "You've done overhangs before."

"What's wrong?" Davis shouted up. His anxious tone hadn't left his voice since she started, pulsing fear up to her with each move she made.

"Nothing. Just picking my path." She would've patted her back at how convincing she sounded if she didn't need both of them to keep from falling to her death.

"I hate this." While he mumbled the words, they still floated up to her.

At least he hadn't argued much with her about climbing up. With the way her head kept spinning, he may have been right. She'd never tell him that, though.

"You know what, Davis?" She dipped her fingertips into the small pouch of chalk she'd packed, determined to get him to stop fretting.

"I'm afraid to ask," he grumbled.

"Your tempting mouth is so much better at kissing than motivation." She peered down and winked.

His low chuckle bounced up the walls to her. She inhaled the sound, letting it fill her with a boost of joy. She shook out her arms and rolled her shoulders. Time to move.

"Sunny, Sunny, she's our gal. If she can't do it, no one shall." Davis's false falsetto burst up the opening.

She jerked with surprise, her foot slipping from its position. Her sides hurt as laughter shook her entire body. Where had this version of Davis come from?

Glancing over her shoulder, Davis stood with his feet planted shoulder-width apart and his arms stoically crossed over his chest. No one would guess he'd just turned cheerleader by the way he stood, which made her laugh even harder. In the eerie light cast from the last glow stick, his lip twitched up. She blew him a kiss and turned back to the climb.

"I didn't know you were a cheerleader."

"All state, senior year." His deadpan answer made her snort.

"Wow. That's impressive." She slid her hand into her

bag to pull another cam out, her fingers walking over the remaining pieces. "Nutcracker."

"Sunny?" His worried tone was back, and she rolled her eyes.

No use telling him about the lack of cams to make it all the way to the top. He'd just freak out more than he already was. And besides, there wasn't anything they could do about it.

"Oh, nothing. Just broke a nail." She left the cam in her bag, surveyed the rock face again, and took a deep breath before reaching for the next handhold.

"You broke a nail?" His feet shuffled, and she could imagine the skepticism splashed across his handsome face.

"Yep." She grunted, wedging her fingers into the tight crack, then leveraging herself up.

"You're something else, Firefly."

"Don't you know it."

She stabilized her feet under her body and stretched herself as far as she could. The handhold was just out of reach. Gritting her teeth, she loosened her fingers from the crack and jumped. Barely brushing a ledge the width of a quarter, she clamped her fingertips over it and grunted when her body jerked against her flexed arm muscles. Her legs swung wide, and her fingers threatened to lose their tenuous hold.

"Sunny! Cam in!" Davis's barked order clambered with the scraping of the rope as it rubbed against the rock.

She aimed her free hand further up the fissure, jamming her fingers in harder than necessary and praying they caught. Her arms burned as her weight tried to pull her off the rock. Lifting with her hands, she fumbled with her feet until they found purchase.

The rough wall grounded her as she rested her forehead against it. All her muscles shook with exertion and adrenaline. She rested two more breaths, then assessed her situation.

"What were you thinking?" Davis's angry question, laced with worry, shot through her tight chest.

"You really need to be quiet right now, Fields." She spoke low, surprised at the bitter irritation coloring her voice.

She pulled on her fingers stuck in the crack. It bit hard and painful but would hold. She sighed, then scanned the rock for a decent place to anchor in. After connecting the cam and hooking in, she examined her bloodied fingers.

"You good?" Davis's soft question balled tension in her throat.

"Yep. Just peachy." She wiped the blood with her shirt as she marked out her next few moves.

"Why the jump?" Davis ground out the words like he spoke through gritted teeth.

"Well, I only have two cams left, and I need to make sure I have one to anchor me beneath the ledge." She dropped her predicament on him without emotion.

Stifling silence spread up and around her, cutting off her air. She forced herself not to look down. All her focus had to be on above.

"You've got this." The truth and belief in his three soft words bolstered her more than any inner encouragement she could come up with.

She nodded, filling her lungs completely full of air, then expelling it with force. Her fingers stung and her thighs burned as she climbed the last twelve feet to the overhang. Before connecting her final cam, she triple-checked the rock face, making sure she chose the correct path. With the cam in, she leaned back on the harness and worked out her muscles.

"Sunny, you're amazing. Scary as all get out, but truly amazing."

As backwards as the compliment was, she relished in it. This man had trained and worked alongside the best the military had. Yet he found her amazing. The last of her frustration at him melted.

"You aren't too bad yourself."

He snorted. "Nothing compared to you."

"Sure. Keep thinking that, Rambo." She flexed her fingers. "Few more feet, then I'll get you out of here."

"Sounds good to me." He cleared his throat. "Nice and slow. No need to rush things."

Only … her burning muscles and weakening fingers claimed otherwise. Not much further and she could rest. Well, after she pulled up their supplies with the other rope, then she could veg for a moment.

She closed her eyes, picturing the handholds she'd picked out, and imagined her path. Reaching her hand to the first ledge, she worked her way up the overhang. When the rock curved down, she tightened her core and let her legs hang free. Davis's pacing below her ratcheted up her anxiety, so she tuned it out by humming Otis Redding. Davis added his voice to her hum, easing her nerves even more. Four walks of her hands up the worst of it, and her feet made purchase.

"Whoop!" she yelled.

"Almost there, babe." Davis's clapping echoed off the walls.

When she reached the top of the opening, the dirt crumbled beneath her hands. Her heart flew into her throat. Falling now would slam her against the rock wall and probably pull out cams. She scrambled against the ledge, snatching at willows to help anchor her as she slid backwards.

Chapter Twenty-Three

Davis's HEART thrashed in his ears as Sunny struggled to clear the edge. His gaze jerked to the cams, then back to her. Would they hold if she lost her grip? She wouldn't survive another drop.

Black spots danced across his vision just as she shimmied the rest of the way up. He collapsed forward, his forearms resting on his knees. Sucking in large gulps of air, he willed his pulse to slow down. When it didn't feel like his chest would explode, he stood and cupped his hands around his mouth.

"Sunny?"

"I'm good."

Her voice barely reached him, but it released the last of his anxiety. At least she'd made it out. He grabbed the few items strewn about and shoved them into his pack. As soon as she recovered, he wanted to be ready. Just as he'd zipped his pack closed, a rope knocked him in the head.

"Oops. Sorry." Sunny's snicker drew his gaze up.

She peered down the hole at him, her chest still

heaving from her exertion. The sun shone behind her, keeping her features shadowed. He'd never seen anything as painfully beautiful as her safely out of that musty tomb.

"You going to hook up the pack or stare at me all day?" She adjusted her stance.

"Firefly, I'd be perfectly content gazing at you for the rest of my life."

"Good, cause I'm thinking we stick together from here on out." Her quick retort pushed the last of the chill from his bones.

"Agreed." He nodded, a big, goofy smile stretching his cheeks in a way that was both foreign and welcome.

"But for now, why don't you get to work?" She wiggled the rope. "I'm thinking a nice, long celebratory make-out session is called for, and I can't do that on my own."

"Yes, ma'am."

He saluted and quickly tied the pack to the rope. After she hauled both packs up, she lowered the harness down for him. He adjusted it to fit and clipped into the rope now secured to the rock wall. With his shoulder spiking pain with each pull, he made the ascent out of the mineshaft.

As he worked his way up the overhang, his arms shook and muscles burned like they were seconds from incineration. He'd climbed a lot of cliffs in his military career, but this one was trickier than all of them combined. It proved, once again, just how tough Sunny was. Maybe he should've settled on a different nick-name, something that encapsulated her strength.

His fingers slipped, and he grunted. Now was not the time to be woolgathering. He tightened his grip and pulled himself up the last and hardest obstacle. When his head poked out of the hole like a meerkat, he was greeted with warm sunlight on his neck and Sunny sitting with her feet pressed against a jutting rock and the rope securing him to the cliff wrapped around her waist.

If he fell, the momentum would catapult her down with him. Only, she wouldn't be strapped in. Murky cold slid along his skin. He scrambled up. When he anchored his fingers in a clump of grass to pull himself up, it yanked loose. He slid backwards, jerking to a halt when she clamped onto his arm.

"Hurry." Her strained voice and wide eyes propelled his feet and hands to scamper the rest of the way out.

She tugged on him, adjusting her grip from his arm to his waist the further he crawled. When he'd made it all the way out, he collapsed to the ground, rolling onto his back. He snaked his good arm around Sunny and rolled her with him so she rested alongside him.

His lungs ached as he sucked in much-needed fresh, crisp air. He ran his hand down her shoulder when she propped herself up, smiled down at him, and laid a long, lingering kiss to his lips. He hadn't had the chance to catch his breath from the exertion of climbing, but he'd take being short-winded if it meant making out with her.

"We made it." She pulled back and stared down at him.

"Yeah." The word croaked out.

Okay, maybe breathing was important. He inhaled, relishing the smell of warm grass. He took another hit, letting the air ease the burn in his lungs.

"You're filthy." She rubbed her finger across his forehead.

"You're gorgeous." He grabbed her hand, concern spiking at the mangled cuts and bruises the climb had created.

He kissed each fingertip, then her palm, and threaded their fingers together and set them on his chest. She sighed, tilting her head to the side and closing her eyes. She huffed out another breath, sat up, and rifled through her pack.

A cool breeze blew, rattling the leaves in the willows surrounding them. The wind tugged on her ponytail. He reached for the twirling strands and ran his fingers through the long, dark length, marveling as the soft strands slipped across his own beaten-up skin. Because of her bravery, they'd gotten out of that hellhole.

He meant it when he'd said he could stare at her forever. They were going to make it. Together, they could secure their survival. He wanted to have her close for years, stretching all the way into eternity.

When she pulled her hand from the pack, she held her InReach. He pushed up off the ground and wrapped his arms around her back, ready to continue that make-out session she'd encouraged him with earlier. He brushed her hair from her shoulder and kissed the back of her neck.

"The InReach still isn't working." She shook her head, disbelief thick like clay.

"Maybe it got damaged." He trailed his lips up her neck toward her ear.

"No. Everything's working. It's just showing no signal whatsoever." She turned to him and shoved the device into his hands. "I've got the best model out there.

This bad boy would work at the North Pole. It *did* work there when Gunnar and Julie called for a pickup. It has *always* connected."

He really didn't want to think about calling out. Right now, he was more interested in celebrating. He groaned, frustrated that she was right.

"More problems or kissing?" He held his hands opened, one balancing the InReach, and moved them up and down like he weighed his options.

"Davis, this is serious." She rolled her eyes.

"So am I." He winked at her.

The lightheartedness normally on her face couldn't be teased out. Her forehead scrunched and face clouded with frustration. She adjusted so she sat on his lap with her legs around him, but the tension didn't leave her muscles. He sighed and surveyed the InReach in his hand. Looked like the celebration would have to wait.

"How is it that it worked perfectly until the day at your camp?" She tapped the device. "It's working, has a full battery and everything. We should get a signal."

He twisted the thing in his hands, examining every side and button while she watched. The thing looked in perfect working order. It was like all the satellites circling the atmosphere had disappeared.

"I've been thinking—"

He groaned at the dread her words conjured.

"No thinking. We just need to move. Get safe." He rubbed the tension in the back of his neck.

"That's the thing. We can't make it all the way to Chicken."

"What do you mean? Of course, we can. We stay low and work our way there." He wasn't about to give up now.

"No, look—" She pulled her pack close and yanked out her map, opening it to the area. "In this terrain, we'll be lucky to make four miles a day. That's if the weather holds." She pointed at the map, dragging her finger to her starred destination. "Chicken is between fifty and sixty miles away. At this rate, it'll take us two weeks to get there if nothing else goes wrong and we don't have to adjust our course to evade the bad guys."

"Sunny, this isn't new intel." He shrugged, not understanding where she was going with all this. "You planned two weeks for the trek. You said so on your video."

Her smile flickered on her face, lighting it up. "You watched that one?"

"I've watched all of them, remember?" He handed her the device back, leaning over to sneak in a quick kiss.

"Focus, Fields. I'm trying to make a point," she complained against his lips, but wrapped her hand around the back of his head and crushed his mouth with so much sizzling heat he'd blister. She yanked away, pushing on his good shoulder for some distance. "You're distracting me."

"I believe you were the one creating the diversion that time." His mouth lifted on one side in a satisfied smirk.

"Don't you smile all sexy like that." She raised her finger in a scold.

"Like what?" He raised his eyebrow and quirked the side of his mouth again.

"Okay, listen. Ugh, I can't think with you so close." She stood abruptly, pacing two steps before spinning back to him. "We need to change our plan."

"So … what? We find a nice, abandoned cabin and hole up for a while? Scavenge berries and roots and shoot small game with a homemade slingshot?" He shrugged as he stood. "More time with you? I'm game."

"No." She tapped on the map. "I think we head to the exploratory mine."

His entire body froze like she had dipped him in the Arctic Ocean.

"Are you nuts?" The words exploded from him, shattering the ice in his veins with hot fear.

"Think about it—"

"Not an option." He spoke over her.

"We're less than five miles away from their facility. They haven't relented in their search for us, and I'm betting they'll expect us to head for Chicken. It's the closest place for help." She stepped toward him, and his entire core trembled with her logic. "The last place they will look for us is at their base. We sneak in, get a message out with a rendezvous location, sneak out, and then wait for the cavalry to arrive."

"We have no clue what we're up against." He grabbed her arms, hoping to talk some sense into her. "You don't have any training in killing people, Sunny. What if I freeze up and can't protect you? You'll get hurt … killed."

"If we get there and it's Fort Knox, then we circle back toward Chicken." She wrapped her fingers around his elbows and squeezed. "But if we can get help in here, if you can contact someone who can bring an army, then Justin's murderers won't get away, and whatever is going on there will be stopped."

Terror burned acid in his throat. This was crazy. He couldn't take her there.

As she stared determinedly into his eyes, dread spun up the acid rolling in his gut to a boil. She would go through with this loco plan. His hands trembled as bloodied images from the past tumbled and mixed with images of her killed. No matter how hard he tried, he couldn't push those thoughts aside, so he did his best to focus on the details she'd laid out.

Chapter Twenty-Four

SUNNY GLANCED BACK at Davis as she trudged through the muskeg. She didn't know what weighed heavier, her heart or her feet. Ever since she'd shifted their course, Davis hadn't spoken more than a grunt or "okay?" He was back to the grump who wouldn't talk to her. Shoot. Every time she caught him watching her, his grief slammed into her chest, like he stared at a dead woman.

Should they just turn around and go to Chicken?

She stepped on a clump of grass, and her foot sunk all the way to her knee, jolting her off balance.

"Stupid muskeg." She growled and lifted her leg with a wet, slurpy *squelch*.

"Okay?" Davis's low question made her eyes blur and nose sting.

No.

No, she wasn't okay. The man she loved wouldn't talk to her. They were walking into the enemy's lair, probably to their doom, and that was all because of her. And now her pants clung, soaking and cold, to her leg.

"I miss the mineshaft."

The words were out before she even thought them through. They were true, though. Trapped in that hole, she'd found hope and belonging in Davis's love.

Davis grunted behind her, and she rolled her eyes, quickly blinking them to dispel the tears. She'd just have to make sure they survived. Then, she'd grab the cantankerous man by the front of the shirt and … and …

And what?

Demand he love her?

Force him to stay with her forever and ever, amen?

She shook her head. This was who she was, blazing through life, helping others and finding adventures that almost always had danger. Just like she went all in with whatever challenge that rose ahead of her, she went all out for the people she cared about.

Shoot.

She even put her all in for people she didn't know. It was the core of her. That was how her ex had duped her so easily, and she had assumed this naïve faith in others was a massive flaw. If she just stayed solo, she could fix it.

But she didn't want to fix it.

Her trusting the good in people, the good in herself, propelled her to risk everything, even her life, for others. It's what made her an excellent guide on the mountain and what gave her the most fulfillment.

She glanced back at Davis, and his tight shoulders and hanging head broadcasted his displeasure. If he couldn't see that what made her shine was her willingness to burn out, incinerate herself for others, then they'd never truly be happy.

And yet, she didn't want to adventure alone anymore.

She wanted to lead people through their wilderness experiences. She longed for Davis to be there beside her, his steady love grounding her, protecting her. But his lack of trust in himself would destroy all that connected them.

She stomped forward, kicking a branch out of her way with more force than necessary. The muskeg gave way to willows, and she pushed through the trees. The branches snagged her hair. Tight trunks closed her in, making it like pushing past prison cell bars. Her pack hung up on a broken branch, and she yanked it through with a frustrated growl.

Misery.

That's what this adventure had turned into. She should've picked a different area, one that might actually be pleasant to slog through … like a Costa Rican jungle along a beach. But then she wouldn't have been here for Davis. He'd have died right alongside Justin, and everyone would have thought their deaths were a tragic accident.

She stumbled as she pushed through a barricade of willows to a clearing. Her foot caught on a downed tree, tripping her. Knees crashing to the ground, she caught herself before she face-planted into a wild raspberry bush. Pain speared through her already beat-up hands.

"Ouch." She groaned as she tried to get up.

Davis's arm wrapped around her waist and hauled her up in a flash. There were definite benefits to having a strong hiking partner. The bush's thorns would've dealt out more injuries if she'd had to struggle up on her own.

When she was on her feet, Davis placed his hand on her cheek, examining her with apprehensive eyes, then gently cupped her hands in his, shifting his scrutiny to her fingers and palms. He pulled a hiss through his teeth and shook his head. Tiny thorns covered her palms.

"You really did a good one." His low, pained words rumbled softly over her, saturating her in guilt.

"Yeah." She swallowed down the overwhelming need to beg him not to be mad. "Hurting myself seems to be a habit."

"Hmm." He tipped his head, motioning behind him. "Let's rest in the cabin and get these cleaned up."

Her gaze darted past him to a tiny structure, half sunk into the earth, that she hadn't noticed when she fell into the clearing. Willows grew around it, hiding it behind green leaves. The back half of the building had sunk a good foot or more into the earth, a common problem with the permafrost. The graying logs and moss-covered roof of the cabin sloped down toward the back, giving the derelict cabin a kind of Dr. Seuss feel. Hopefully, the inside wasn't overrun with vermin. Sleeping in there would hide them better than her bright tent.

She followed Davis to the structure, exhaustion turning her legs into wet noodles. They clomped onto the warped boards set up as a makeshift porch. He turned the homemade handle, but the door made from birch logs didn't open. Her sigh came all the way from her toes.

"Is it locked?" She shifted her pack, wondering why anyone would lock a cabin way out here, especially with the Alaskan bush hospitality code: use the cabin, but leave it better than you found it.

"Just stuck."

Davis rammed his shoulder into the wood. It creaked but didn't budge. That door was solid as all get-out, and him banging on it would only get him hurt.

"We can just camp out here on the porch." She scanned the tilting roof.

It looked sturdy enough. Davis slammed his body against the door again. The roof jerked, raining dirt down on her. She blinked and shook her hair out.

"Davis, this whole thing is going to come down if you keep it up." Sunny bunched her muscles, preparing to jump to safety if the roof crashed down on them.

"Just one more …"

Davis's next ram produced a loud scraping of wood on wood. The door opened half a foot. He wrapped his fingers around the door's edge and gave it a push, screeching it loose further. She peeked in around his shoulder, then followed him in.

The inside smelled of decaying wood and fabric. The furnishings were sparse and handmade, only a table with two chairs and a twin bed. Two shelves hung on the walls. One over a makeshift counter had a few canned goods and a stack of dishes. A handful of books lined the other shelf.

She walked toward the bookshelf, smiling at how the floor sloped toward the back of the cabin, then disappeared into the ground it sank into. Louis L'amour titles mixed with old Alaskan plant and homesteading guides.

"Here, come sit next to the window." Davis checked the chairs and tables for stability.

She pulled her pack's strap off her shoulder, hissing as the thorns scraped against the fabric. With the next strap, she wiggled her arm to get it free and let the pack drop to the floor with a *thunk*. She sat in the chair, her plop sounding a lot like her pack had.

Davis dug out the first-aid kit and laid it out on the table. The other chair scraped as he dragged it beside hers. Without a word, he took her hand and bent over it with the tweezers. She jerked with each thorn he yanked out. He blew on the skin, and she closed her eyes to the sensation. She didn't think it actually helped with the pain, but it was such a caring action that it eased her muscles. He kissed her palm, and she opened her eyes.

"Next." His raw voice scraped against her heart.

He didn't like causing her pain. She smiled wearily as she handed him her other hand. His eyebrows bunched as he looked at the more mangled hand. With her good hand, she ran her fingers through his hair. He'd let the top grow long since last spring, and it curled wildly around his ears and down his neck.

"Sunny, you're a mess."

"Yeah, pretty much." She dropped her hand and stared out the grimy window the table was pushed under.

He cleared his throat. She could feel his stare on her, but she couldn't look at him. There was no way she could handle the disappointment she'd see there. Not right now when everything hurt and exhaustion pulled at her. Silence stretched between them as he continued to doctor her hand. The fireweed waved in the breeze, their purply-pink blossoms blurring in her unfocused gaze.

"Done." Davis pressed another kiss to her palm. "All better."

"Thanks." She flexed her palm at the throbbing ache.

"Listen—"

The beep of her InReach, clipped to her pack, snapped both of their attentions to it. She scrambled from the chair, and her knees almost buckled at the icon showing they had service. Thrusting the device at Davis, she bounced with the jolt of energy.

"You send for help first."

She clasped her hands together and pressed them to her mouth, silently praying they'd get a message out. His fingers raced over the buttons. When he pressed send and the confirmation tone beeped, she had to tighten her knees to keep from collapsing.

"Text your family." He handed the InReach to her.

Just as she typed her message, the connection dropped.

"What?" She shook it. "No, you stupid thing."

She pressed the message and hit send just in case. Nothing. Growling, she darted her gaze to Davis.

"Why would it do that? It makes no sense."

Davis's eyes widened. He jerked his head to look out the window. His jaw clenched.

"Get your gear." His words fired out. "We have to leave."

"Why?" she asked, but she didn't wait for the answer to lift her pack.

"I'm not sure. Gut feeling." Davis packed up the first-aid kit and pushed her toward the door. "You can't pinpoint a signal if it's not working."

Her steps froze on the porch as what he said fully registered. If their enemy could somehow track their signal, then Davis's message just gave their location away.

"Why wouldn't they just keep it on then? Find us quicker?" She turned to him.

"We'd be able to get messages out to the authorities. This way, they know where to start looking." He stepped up to her, squeezing her elbow. "Don't worry. We'll make clear tracks south toward Chicken, then circle back. I won't let them find us."

She nodded, swallowing the lump of fear choking her. She may act tough, declaring their need to infiltrate enemy lines. But if these guys had tech this sophisticated, her and Davis's sneaking might lead them right into destruction.

Chapter Twenty-Five

Davis checked under the overhang for animals. When he found none, he motioned Sunny inside, then crawled in behind her. The dirt above should protect them from being seen on heat sensors, and, even if it didn't, they needed to stop. They'd walked another two hours after leaving the cabin, and they were both past exhausted.

A helicopter had sounded by the cabin's location, touching down a mere twenty minutes after their message had sent. His only consolation was that the *whump-whump* of the rotors, once the bird took back to the air, had headed away from them after circling for several minutes. Hopefully, that meant they'd fallen for his fake trail.

"Aah, musty dirt." Sunny sighed as she took her pack off and set it against the roots hiding the opening. "Feels like home."

The small space wasn't any bigger than the first overhang they'd hidden under. There would barely be enough space to stretch out in. Didn't matter. He was so tired he could probably sleep standing.

She pulled the sleeping bag out of her pack and laid it out in the dirt. Dark circles bruised the skin under her eyes. None of the spark that drew him to her flashed.

This trip would destroy her.

It would've been better if she'd never stumbled on their camp. Sure, he'd be dead right alongside Justin. But at least she'd be safe.

Maybe, if he worded it right, he could convince her to stay here. He'd scout ahead to the mine, sneak in, then be back without having to put her in any more danger than necessary. He ran his hand through his hair as his stomach quivered.

She'd never go for it.

But he had to try.

She crawled into the sleeping bag, then patted the tiny space of fabric next to her with a hesitant smile. Any other time, he'd be clambering to hold her. Shoot. Even now, he wanted to wrap her in his arms and never let go. Holding her would only make what he had to say harder.

"Tomorrow, can I convince you to stay here while I scout ahead?" He scanned past the roots blocking their hiding spot so he didn't have to see her reaction.

"You're nuts." Even her disagreement didn't hold spunk. It just frayed the air with thready exhaustion. "I'm not letting you go alone."

"I'll be better on my own. I've snuck into enemy camps more times than I can remember." He finally looked at her. "It's Infiltrating 101. The fewer bodies moving, the less chance of getting caught."

She snorted and shook her head. "Nice try, but no. I may not be a super soldier, but I've successfully snuck up on more animals bow hunting than *I* can remember."

She propped herself up with her arm, tipping her head to the side. "Do you know how hard it is to get close enough to a dall sheep to shoot it with an arrow? I can guarantee it's a lot harder than sneaking up on a person."

"Sunny, please." He'd beg if he had to.

"Davis, it's not gonna happen." She lay back down. "Look, we're both exhausted. Can we please get some sleep?"

He clenched his jaw. The force spiked pain up to his temples as he jerked his gaze back down the hill. The Rebels and their stubbornness. Were any of them conciliatory? He peeked back at her, and she lifted her eyebrow in challenge.

Probably not.

Mulishness ran thick in their blood.

He growled and stretched out beside her on his back, crossing his arms over his chest.

"Stubborn." She pressed her face against his shoulder.

"Glad you recognize that about yourself."

Her weak huff of a laugh broke his heart. Before all of this, she would've been poking at him or tickling him … anything that she could in mock defense. Now, she couldn't even laugh fully.

He closed his eyes as they grew hot. She shifted beside him. Her lips pressed gently against his neck before she settled her face back to his arm.

"Get some sleep, soldier." She whispered the command with a tired sigh.

"Yes, ma'am."

He uncrossed his arms and gave in to the need to hold her. With his arm around her back, she melded to his side. This time, her sigh filled the musty space with contentment.

"I love you, Davis." She draped her arm across his middle and settled her head over his heart. "No matter what happens, I want you to know that."

No matter what happens.

The exhaustion morphed into a heavy, dull pain throughout his body. She wasn't as confident with their crazy plan, either. A tear escaped, racing across his skin and pooling in his ear. He didn't wipe it away, just tightened his arms around her so that no space remained between them. She wouldn't see his weakness, anyway.

"I love you too, Firefly."

It hurt to push the words out of his tight throat. Hurt to have this much hope when it came to her, yet so many insurmountable obstacles to make that hope reality. For longer than he should have, he laid awake, cherishing the fleeting feeling of her in his arms.

Chapter Twenty-Six

SUNNY FOLLOWED Davis through the forest in the early morning mist, picking her movements with careful deliberation. They'd skirted Justin's homestead a few miles back and closed in on the exploratory mining site. Davis had them stash most of their gear in a cluster of thick fireweed next to the clearing Justin's family had used for a makeshift airstrip. If Davis could contact help, the field was the perfect place to rendezvous. Near enough, but not so close the approaching aircraft would be heard.

The bear spray hanging from her belt rattled against a branch, the loud metallic clang foreign in the birdsong and bug buzzing. Sweat pooled in her pits. She clamped her hand over the can, pressing it against her leg.

Davis held up a fist, just like in those action movies her brothers always watched. She froze, her muscles bunching to run or hide or whatever Davis told her to do. He leaned to the side with such a slow, steady movement that a sloth would beat him in a race. Her heart pounded so hard in her chest she could feel it in her throat.

She was not cut out for this super commando stuff.

He moved backward toward her, never taking his eyes off what he'd spotted through the trees. Part of her wanted to sneak up past him and look, just to know what had her limbs trembling in fear. The bigger part wanted to do a one-eighty and dash back through the woods they had just come through. Since neither would help them, she stayed rooted like a spindly black spruce, stationary, but one little push would send her toppling.

He stepped up to her, wrapping his hand around her hip and pulling her up against him. She gripped his shirt in her fingers, the quaking rushing through her body calming with his nearness. He bent close, finally turning his gaze from what he'd found.

His breath tickled her ear a moment before he spoke so low she almost couldn't hear. "Facility just through the trees. We'll find a hiding place. Follow close."

He pulled back enough to stare into her eyes, his intensity silently asking if she understood. She nodded, hoping her fear wasn't blinking on her face like a neon sign. His lips twitched in a sad smile before he pecked a kiss on her mouth.

She mimicked his every move as he led them in a circle through the thick spruce around the facility. Every now and then, she'd catch sight of the equipment, but the trees grew so tightly together, they revealed little. She hated traversing through the grabby, close-growing trees, but the dense, overlapping branches hid their movements.

After thirty minutes of circling, Davis crouched and crawled beneath one of the larger spruces. She followed, quickly recognizing the man's genius. Underneath, moss blanketed the ground, while on the side facing the facility, a dead willow crisscrossed the opening like lattice. Their bodies sank into the moss, concealing them better than if they'd settled on dirt. She released her tension into the soft cushion.

She settled herself close to Davis, leaning her mouth right next to his ear. "You are one smart man, Davis Fields."

Her lips grazed his skin as she spoke, sending a shiver of delight through her. She pulled back, because making out during a stakeout definitely was against the rules. His broad smile, full of confidence, had her grinning in return.

Before she kissed the living daylights out of the man and gave away their location, she turned her attention to the complex. She scanned the cleared area, surprised that it looked like exactly what it was supposed to be. A drill towered above the ground, surrounded by a network of scaffolding that reminded her of oil drills from the old western movies her dad loved. A series of connected metal shipping containers with windows cut into the side and a door cut into the end, sat a hundred yards away from the drill. That, most likely, held the offices or the barracks. Maybe both. A large, open canvas tent had been erected next to the containers and had picnic tables and a cooking area in it. A handful of all-terrain vehicles lined the opposite side of the forest.

That was it.

Nothing spectacular or nefarious looking.

A door slammed, jerking her attention to the building. A man crossed to the tent while buttoning up a flannel shirt over a protruding belly. He ducked into the tent, and pots and pans clanging quickly filled the quiet morning. Not long after, more men filtered out of the building and headed to the drill. A generator roared to life, and soon the rhythmic *thunk, thunk* of the drill vibrated the ground beneath her.

The entire scene confused her.

Where were the devious men?

Why was everything so open and unassuming?

"I don't get it," she whispered to Davis, confident the busyness of the mine would cover her voice. "There's no fencing, no guards. If they're up to something, wouldn't they be more—I don't know—cautious?"

"Why would they? There's no one for miles, and if they put up a bunch of fencing and guards, it might raise red flags when inspectors come."

He brought the binoculars to his face and scanned the area. She had no clue what he was scanning for. Nothing was there. They hadn't even seen Zhang or the twisted duo in the milling of people.

After watching the men amble around, heading to the tent for breakfast, then returning to the drill, she came to the understanding that stakeouts sucked. Mosquitos buzzed all around her, spearing her with their teeny needles of torture, yet she couldn't swat at them. She itched, her protein bar all but disappeared in her belly, and she'd never been so bored in her life. Worse thing was Davis's nonchalant statement at the start of the stakeout that they'd be there until everyone went to bed.

The only consolation to this horrible day was her ability to stare at Davis as he stayed vigilant beside her. She'd studied him for the last hour. Honestly, he was by far the most interesting thing out there.

Even taking in his handsome face didn't stop her eyes from drooping. She felt her body relaxing more fully into the moss, and she jerked herself awake. Blinking her eyes to put some energy into them, she huffed out a frustrated breath. Davis turned his inspection to her, his eyes softening in understanding.

"It's okay, Firefly." He reached out and brushed his thumb over her eyes, then the back of his fingers down her cheeks. "Sleep. I'll keep watch."

Her eyelids weighed as much as a moose as she tried to keep them open.

"Guess I'm not a great stakeout partner after all," she whispered as her eyes closed.

"You're the best partner I've ever had." His lips pressed against hers. "Most beautiful too."

She sighed at the compliment. A smile twitched on her lips when she thought of men like her brothers or the Stryker Security team cuddled up under a tree with Davis. Okay, she'd just rest for a minute, then she'd get back to business.

Chapter Twenty-Seven

Lips pressed against Sunny's, their touch soft and tentative. Her pulse thudded in her ears, drowning all other sounds. Warmth covered her, and she blinked. Light shone brightly, making everything hard to see except the man before her.

Davis.

Gosh, he was beautiful. Laugh lines bracketed his eyes. A smile not tarnished with worry stretched across his face.

"Wake up, sleepyhead."

He kissed her again, drawing the touch out until her fingers curled into his shirt and the pounding in her ears quickened like a competitive drum line. When he finally pulled away, her vision focused. She glanced around.

Where were they?

Open blue sky replaced the black spruce branches. Wildflowers swayed in the breeze. In the distance, Mount Denali graced the horizon, which made no sense.

"Come on, Firefly, it's time to wake up."

Davis gently shook her shoulder. She blinked. The dream faded to Davis leaning over her. Black spruce limbs crisscrossed behind him, eerie green moss hanging from the sickly branches. A shiver of dread raced along her neck, covering her skin in goosebumps. A line of worry slashed between his eyes.

Would she ever have that dream, or would it die in the Alaskan wilderness like so many others?

Her eyes stung, and she blinked. Davis's mouth tightened even more in concern. She smiled broadly, hoping to play off her distress, grabbed the back of his neck, and kissed him with all the passion the dream had given her, though her heart was heavy with hopelessness. He didn't hesitate, matching her desperation with his own. His weight pressed her into the moss and burned away the icy fear. She wrapped her arms around him and fisted the back of his shirt.

Much too soon, he pulled away. His ragged breathing skated across her skin. She unclenched her fists and smoothed the fabric of his shirt over his muscles that jumped with her touch.

"Yeah. That definitely hasn't happened on a stakeout before." He chuckled, kissing her one more time before rolling off her with a huff.

"That's good." She turned over, propped herself on her elbows, and scanned the darkened clearing. "I mean, I've met your friends, and I don't think they'd have responded the same."

"No. No, they wouldn't." He chuckled low again, and she relished the sound.

Swallowing the lump in her throat, she nodded toward the empty opening. "What time is it?"

The sky had the dark, dusk blue with oranges and pinks threading in the west.

"It's one. No movement for the last hour, so it's time to go snooping."

She snapped her gaze to where he still laid on his back. "I slept that long?"

He shrugged. "You were exhausted."

"But … what about you?" How could she have been that out of it? "You're just as tired."

"I caught a few z's. I'm good." He levered himself up and kissed her again. "Ready?"

She nodded. "No."

He smiled against her lips, kissed her one last time, and tapped her on the hip. "Let's go, sleepyhead."

They backed out of their hiding spot and worked their way through the forest toward the temporary building. A wolf howled in the distance, turning her fingers to ice. Another answered the call, the long mournful sound piercing the still, silent night.

She would not let the noise get to her.

Gritting her teeth, her eyes darted to the dark woods.

She wouldn't.

Davis stopped at the edge of the trees and motioned her forward. "Stay close."

He didn't have to tell her twice. She grabbed the back of his shirt and stayed practically glued to him as they darted across the clearing to the connex door. Her gaze frantically scanned the empty yard, the trees, and the drill for the bad guys waiting to jump out and ambush them. The quiet area felt like a trap.

They tiptoed up the metal stairs to the door, and she cringed with each tap and creak. Davis stood to the handle side of the door and pushed her behind him. Holding her breath while she peeked through the space between him and the building, the handle turned in his hand. She gasped, then covered her mouth.

She guessed it made sense. Why lock doors when your evil lair was in the middle of nowhere?

Davis cracked open the door with a metallic screech, did his military commando scan, then nodded once.

"Clear."

His low word, like she was actually one of his squad members, made her smile. Her amusement was totally inappropriate. She pressed her lips together to keep from giggling. Had the stress of the situation melted her brain?

He grabbed her hand and pulled her into the building as the unmistakable *thump-thump* of a fast-approaching helicopter filled the night air. A door slammed in another part of the connex. Davis froze, pulling her up against his back like a shield and pressing her into the wall. She counted, trying to regulate her breaths to the numbers so she wouldn't hyperventilate. Thirty-seconds later, a shadow crossed outside the window.

The temporary building shuddered as the helicopter landed. Davis threaded her fingers through his and eased down the hall with windows on one side and doors on the other. He opened the first door. His penlight clicked on and scanned, the light grazing over cleaning supplies, then just as quickly clicked off. The next door held food, the following a bathroom.

Boots clanged on the metal stairs leading to the exterior door. Angry voices accompanied the stomping. She darted her gaze back, then forward. The next door was spaced farther away than the previous ones. They wouldn't make it. Her chest ached from her heart's battering attempt to escape out of her ribs.

Davis yanked her down the hallway. His silent footsteps were quick and sure compared to her clumsy ones. He reached the door and pushed her in just as the heavy door at the end of the hall screeched open.

Sunny scanned the dark but couldn't make out anything. Davis set her up against the wall next to the door with him in front of her, once again acting like a shield. She didn't want him to be their sole protection. Unclipping her bear spray, she slid it out nice and slow, so it didn't make a noise.

Heavy footsteps pounded down the hall. *Please don't come in here. Please don't come in here.* She willed the men to just keep walking.

"How hard can it be to find two idiot miners?" It was that Zhang guy, and his raging voice exploded into the quiet.

"There's a lot of wilderness out there, boss," Justin's shooter answered.

She clenched her teeth as anger burned hot in her throat.

"You think I don't know that? It's why we're testing here." Zhang's angry approach stopped.

"Of course, sir. Sorry." Shooter stammered. "I just meant they can't get to help for at least a couple of weeks on foot. We'll find them."

"You better." The threat sent a shiver down her spine.

A throat cleared, but Shooter's voice still shook. "The pilot should be done filling up. But … well … well, the thing is, sir, he's exhausted. Seeing double. Says he needs a break before he crashes."

The pause lasted so long, Sunny wondered if Zhang was making good on his promise to kill the shooter if he failed. She tried not to picture the boss strangling the man, but in the dark, her imagination ran wild. Closing her eyes to listen for struggling didn't help.

"Fine." Zhang's low, menacing answer almost made her knees buckle. "Eight hours. That's all he gets."

"Got it."

Tentative footsteps moved back toward the outside door before they quickened to almost a run. Muttered curses filled the hall as Zhang stomped toward their door. He stopped just outside their hiding spot and roared expletives. She slapped her hand over her mouth to keep from screaming, her heart about to break loose.

Chapter Twenty-Eight

DAVIS SHIFTED HIS STANCE, preparing to attack Zhang the instant he opened the door. Another harsh curse exploded from behind the thin wood. A fist pounded on the wall next to Davis's ear before Zhang's stomping continued down the hall. With the slam of a door in the distance, Davis relaxed.

"Holy moly." Sunny's voice shook as she sagged against the wall. "How many years did you put yourself through situations like this?"

"Too many."

Davis leaned his forehead on the wall and took a calming breath to ease his shaking. For now, they were safe. They needed to move if they wanted to stay that way.

"You okay?" He clicked on the penlight, and Sunny's ashen face and wide eyes stared at him.

"Right as rain." Her smile was so forced even a child could call her bluff.

"Good."

If she wanted to pretend everything was fine, he

would too. She didn't need to know he'd never been more afraid he'd fail and she'd get captured and killed than those last moments. Better for her to think he had all the confidence in the world. Under any other circumstance, this would be another day at work, but with her life at stake, the pressure not to screw up had him more on edge than ever.

He turned his light to the room, more relief rushing through his muscles at the bank of computers and desks up against a solid wall. Finally, a room they could use. Hopefully, what they needed would be here. He wrapped his hand around her wrist.

"Stay close to the door and listen for anyone approaching." He didn't want her that exposed, but he couldn't be in two places at once. "Keep the spray in your hand."

She nodded, her shoulders rolling as she pushed off from her slump against the wall.

He eyed a SAT phone on one desk and rushed to it. The device had a full battery, but no service, just like Sunny's InReach.

He turned his attention to the computers, touching the mouse pads to see if any were still on. The second to last one's screen flashed light into the room. Data ran in some kind of reporting program.

"The SAT phone isn't working?" Sunny shuffled through binders stacked on a table.

"Nope."

"Jinkies! It looks like we've got ourselves a mystery." Sunny's reference to Scooby-Doo made him smile.

"Ruh, Ruh." Davis did his best Scooby-Doo impression, which wasn't very good.

Sunny snickered and pulled her bottom lip between her teeth. "Scooby fan?"

"More like lots of downtime in the military. There's almost always re-runs of that show on."

"So, how are we going to get help if communication is down here too?"

Davis slid into the seat in front of the computer and clicked around. "Hopefully, their computers are set up to a secure network or something."

While she went back to flipping through the papers, he pulled up the internet browser. When a plain page with the mine's logo opened, Davis sat back in surprise. He hadn't expected it to work. He quickly recovered and typed the secure communications line Rafe had set up for Stryker Security Force.

"Please work. Please work. Please work." He prayed as he clicked return.

The secure login page popped open.

"Yes. Finally."

The air rushed from his lungs. They would get help.

He entered his login information, his eyes stinging when Rafe's "Welcome to Rafe's Super Secret and Totally Awesome Communication Center" filled the screen. Davis had never been so happy to see Rafe's idiotic words before. As he clicked on the phone icon, his leg bounced in nervous anticipation. Would the call go through?

"Davis, where are you?" Rafe's voice didn't hold any of its usual joviality.

"Man, we're in trouble."

"Tell me something I don't know." Rafe forced a laugh.

"I'm here with Sunny Rebel. Justin's been murdered, and we're on the run."

"What?" Voices exploded in the background.

"Shut it!" Rafe yelled. "Let the man speak."

"There's this exploratory mine not far from Justin's, but, man, there's something fishy going on up here." Davis shook his head. "The murderers are here. Sunny and I need a pick up, but we also need the authority to take down these guys."

"We're here at the Rebel's place getting ready to head to the location of your transmission. Bjørn just finished his pre-flight check. We have the local troopers with us, and we'll be airborne in less than ten," Rafe reported.

Davis glanced at Sunny as she sucked in a shaky breath. Her lashes fluttered, trying to clear her glassy eyes. A tear escaped anyway, and she dashed it off her cheek with the back of her hand. She was so strong, this firefly of his.

"Listen, these guys have some crazy tech up here." He turned his focus back to Rafe, needing to get off this call and out of there. "If we want to get the drop on them, we'll have to come in quiet. Sunny and I have a rendezvous point that's a few miles out. Bjørn will have to dust off his Nightstalker skills, though, and come in low and quiet."

"Dude, my skills are spot on. You just focus on keeping my sister safe and leave the flying to me." Bjørn's voice, while joking, had a tightness to it that exposed his worry.

"Copy that." Davis gave the location and signed off, deleting the evidence they'd used the computer.

"Davis," Sunny hissed his name and clicked off her light.

He put the screen to sleep, sending the windowless room into complete darkness, and slipped over to the door. Sunny's hands trembled as she placed them on his back. Tired footsteps clomped down the hall.

"Glad we can rest. I can't even keep my eyes open."

"Yeah," Shooter said. "Just don't forget to set your alarm. Zhang's not kidding about the eight hours. If we're not in the air, we're both dead."

"I can't wait for the testing phase to be done, and we can move to other areas," the pilot grumbled as they passed outside the door. "I'm hoping to be stationed far away from that psycho."

Shooter snorted. "No joke."

What did they mean "other areas"? Davis's mind circled, but he shut the questions down. They had to get to the rendezvous point, but first, he wanted to do a little helicopter maintenance. Five minutes later, as he darted northwest through the forest with Sunny close behind, he chuckled in satisfaction, hoping he got to see Zhang's face when the man's world burst wide open.

Chapter Twenty-Nine

Sunny rubbed her arms in the chilly night air. Knowing the mine's helicopter wouldn't be searching for them, they'd made it back to the coordinates in record time. She shivered. The exertion had worked up a sweat, and Alaskan summer nights held little heat.

Davis stepped up behind her and wrapped his arms around her shoulders. "Cold?"

"Sweaty."

"Ew."

He went to let go, but she grabbed his arms with one hand and elbowed him in the side with the other. His laugh held relief she hadn't heard since this entire fiasco started. As he bent to her neck, she leaned her head to the side, relishing the warmth of his body wrapped around her. He placed his face against her skin and breathed in. Another shiver rushed through her body, but this time the sensation spread heat instead of cold.

"I take it back." He kissed her neck. "You don't smell bad."

"Doubt that." She leaned against him, hugging his

arms to her. "Especially with not showering, being stuck in a mineshaft, and steeped in fear."

"Trust me. Compared to some missions I've been on with big smelly men, you aren't too bad." He took another whiff. "The forest clings to you."

They stood there in the clearing. The sun lit the eastern sky pink after its brief dip below the northern horizon. She could easily pretend everything was normal, easily let Alaska cleanse her of the horror the last days had held, at least for the minutes that stretched while they waited. But questions kept circling, invading the pseudo-peace the midnight sun created.

"What do you think they meant by 'other places'?" She whispered the question blaring loudest in her head, hating the tremor she couldn't hide.

"I've been wondering the same thing." He squeezed her closer, like he wanted to shield her even in this quiet place.

"One of those binders had diagrams for the drill. It struck me as odd since there's really not many changes you can make to one." She shook her head, confused all over again by page after page of schematics. "I mean, equipment like that doesn't change."

"When we capture the facility, we'll figure it out. Whatever it is they're hiding won't stay hidden much longer." He kissed the top of her head.

"Do you think the team will surprise them, take them down without a fight?"

How she prayed it would be. She didn't want anymore pain. Didn't want another death to rip her soul open.

"I hope so, but—"

Sunny didn't like how Davis's sentence cut off.

"But what? What aren't you telling me?" She went to turn, but he held her tight against him with a heavy sigh.

"The first room wasn't just a supply closet. It held a locked armory behind the door. If they see us coming, they'll fight."

She squeezed her eyes shut. Hopefully, the mine would still be deep in sleep. She glanced at her watch, her hope evaporating. By the time the cavalry arrived and they made a plan, it would be pushing five. The camp had roused at five-thirty the day before. That didn't give the team a lot of wiggle room.

"What's your plan?"

"You think I have one?" Davis chuckled.

"I know you do. You're too smart not to have one, and probably two or three back-up ones set up in your head."

"Such faith." His awe-filled whisper broke her heart.

If only he would trust himself again. She turned in his arms and wrapped hers around his neck. His hands spread wide across her back, pulling her tight against him.

"I trust you, Davis. One hundred percent. You're going to get us out of this, because you and I are going to have a long life together finding adventures and, one day, sharing those adventures with our children."

"Sunny, I—" His loud swallow filled her ears.

"It's Firefly, and I don't know if you caught that, soldier, but just in case, let me spell it out." She pushed onto her toes and put her mouth so her lips brushed his when she talked. "I want to marry you, find our place in the world together, and have a houseful of beautiful babies. What do you think about that?"

"A houseful?" he whispered in the quiet.

"Big house, at that." She speared her fingers through his hair.

He smiled against her lips. "A life full of your light?" He kissed her softly and leaned his forehead to hers. "That's all I've wanted since we first met. I just don't know if I—"

"Don't you even say it, Davis Fields." She placed the fingertips of one hand over his mouth, her voice quivering with the force of her indignation. "You deserve happiness. You deserve light and joy. What happened to your team wasn't your fault. You don't have to carry that guilt anymore."

Just like she didn't have to carry the embarrassment of her failure. His eyes searched hers, and his doubt tore at her. But, banked behind the doubt, hope peeked through, muted like the pinks and oranges coloring the sky. If they could both trust each other and, in that trust, find faith in themselves, the long, dark winter they'd both been in could give way to a bright summer. She didn't want to be alone anymore, and she would not let him be alone, either.

"I'm going to try to put that weight down, Firefly."

He kissed her, long and slow. His touch full of promises and love. She answered in kind, pouring her own vows of love into each caress. She'd do all that she could to help him shoulder that weight until he could fully put it aside. It'd be a long trail. She'd seen that with her dad and siblings, but that's what loving a person who served in the military meant.

"So?" She pulled back as the soft *thump-thump* of a fast-approaching helicopter broke the night silence.

"So?" He laughed against her lips. "You've addled my brain."

"We doing life together or not, soldier?"

"Yes, ma'am, I accept your proposal." He seared her with a crushing kiss, pulling back much too quickly. "There is no way I'm letting you go now."

"Good."

The rotors whipped the air around them. She kissed Davis one more time, then buried her face in his neck to block the wind. He covered her head with his arms and turned so his back was to the landing helicopter. Before the engine cut off, her name yelled in anguished relief crashed over her.

She peeked over Davis's shoulder in time to watch Gunnar jump from the helicopter before it touched down. Her stoic brother's eyebrows slashed his forehead with worry. She pushed away from Davis and ran to meet Gunnar. He wrapped her in his arms, a sob shaking his body.

"Thank God." His words, laced with tears, pushed her own to breach the surface. "You're okay?"

"Yeah." She nodded, not able to say anymore.

The engine cut, and Bjørn's yell followed. "Sunny!"

He was pulling her from Gunnar's arms before the rotors stopped spinning. His body shook, too, as he squeezed her tight. She glanced at Davis as Gunnar embraced him in a back-thumping hug. Relief washed over her. They'd be all right now. They had to be.

/ Chapter Thirty

"ABOUT A HALF-CLICK FROM THE MINE, we'll split into two teams to circle the facility." Davis pointed to the map to indicate the directions each team would go. "After that, Sunny will get into her hiding spot, then the rest of us will close in."

"I don't like it." Bjørn slashed his hand through the air, and Davis had to admit he agreed with the man.

"Absolutely not." Gunnar crossed his arms over his chest and scowled.

"It's a good plan." Rafe countered the opposition, and Davis clenched his teeth to keep his emotions in against the relief of having his team, all the Stryker family, here with him.

Davis bristled anyway. Laying out the plan of attack had gone well until he revealed the part that clenched his stomach with worry. He didn't want Sunny anywhere near the fight. Now, he wondered if giving in to her brothers' objections was smarter than going with his plan.

"Davis is right." Sunny crossed her arms, a beautiful and determined reflection of her brother. "It's not safe for me to stay here. If their helicopter gets airborne, I'm a sitting duck here with Bjørn's helicopter."

Yes, there definitely was that possibility. The bigger issue was Davis had known Sunny would refuse to be left behind. So, rather than try to force her to stay and then worry about her following, he'd found a way that he hoped she'd approve of.

"But you're even more of a sitting duck close to the fight." Bjørn pointed toward the mine.

"No. I'll be hiding far enough from the fight that the chances of being found are slim, especially with me hiding north instead of south, where anyone escaping will most likely go. Trust me. I don't want to be part of the fight." Sunny shuddered and rolled her shoulders. "But I'm not waiting this far away while you take them down."

"We don't have any more Super Suits. You'll be completely unprotected." Gunnar paced away, then stomped back.

He referred to the bulletproof suits the Stryker team had brought along. The special fabric deflected bullets in a way that Davis still didn't understand but completely respected. The team hadn't expected to need so many, but with the Rebel men and the state troopers, the extra suits were currently occupied. Since Sunny had called Davis an idiot with a roll of her eyes when he had insisted she wear his, he'd pulled his on, though everything in him wanted to hold her down and have her brothers stuff her into the protection.

That wouldn't build trust, though, would it?

"You all are being idiots." Sunny threw her arms up, and Davis was glad he wasn't the only one she called that. "We need to get going, now. So, unless you want to tie me down, therefore putting a big heat-producing flag for the bad guys, we're done with the conversation." She pushed past the men and stomped toward the facility. "You coming?"

Davis lifted an eyebrow at the Rebel brothers with a chuckle. "She's a firecracker, all right."

He jogged after her.

"Darn Rebel muleheadedness," Bjørn muttered, but his footsteps followed.

Davis overtook Sunny. She winked at him as he passed, but her smile looked strained. When the team was half a mile out from the facility, he motioned them to split. Half of his friends slowed and disappeared into the heavy woods. The rest followed him left. They'd converge on the enemy from the north and west, limiting the chance of crossfire.

"In position." Rafe's voice whispered in Davis's com.

"Copy," Davis replied, his breath whooshing out that the devices worked.

What could keep communication down, but not the earpieces? Did it have to do with satellites? He shook off the questions and pulled short at a cutback in the hill he had spotted when he and Sunny had retreated earlier.

"There." He pointed to the small space hidden by a cluster of willows growing along the creek following the base of the hill.

"It'll do." Sunny nodded.

Doubt skidded along his skin. "I wish it was high on the hill like our other spots, but—"

"Davis, it'll work. There's enough of an overhang that if I hear the helicopter taking off, I can easily tuck myself under it." She stepped close and grabbed his arm. "I'll be fine. I'll just wait here and listen as you take these guys down."

He touched her ear where the com nestled, then trailed his fingers to the mic around her neck so she could call in help if needed. He closed his eyes and leaned his forehead on hers. This was wrong, leaving her here unprotected.

"I have my gun and my pepper spray," she whispered like she'd read his mind. "I'll be fine. Go finish this so we can start those adventures."

"I love you, Firefly." He slid his fingers into her hair.

"I love you too." She grabbed the front of his shirt and kissed him with a desperation he felt all the way to his soul, then pushed him away. "Go."

He took her in, her dark eyes shining a trust he still wasn't sure he deserved. One he was determined to live up to. He swallowed down all his doubts balling in his throat, and, with a nod, turned from his light to face darkness once again.

"When this is done, we're talking." Gunnar's cheek popped as Davis passed.

"A nice, long talk about intentions and all that stuff," Bjørn added his input.

"Won't take long at all." Davis looked from one brother to the next. "I'm marrying your sister as soon as we can arrange a ceremony. I can't live without her, and so I won't."

He clapped Bjørn on the shoulder as he passed.

"Well, that went well." Bjørn's voice sounded a little

disappointed, like maybe he was looking forward to interrogating Davis.

Gunnar grunted. "Darn shame."

Davis let his smile go as he slipped through the forest. One thing was for sure, he'd never met a family like the Rebels. He couldn't wait to be a part of it.

Chapter Thirty-One

Sunny paced along the creek bank as the whispered positions of the team tickled her ear through the com. Maybe being away from the fight wasn't the best idea. She didn't want to see it, but she also vibrated with anxiety.

"Ready?" Davis's voice asked.

Sunny clenched her collar, pulling the choking fabric from her tight throat. Clicking in her ear, the signal that all were ready, turned her blood to ice. *Please.* She couldn't pray any more than that as she strained to hear gunfire.

"Contact." A sharp whisper through the com jerked her muscles.

She squeezed her eyes shut to her useless tears. "Oh, please, please, please."

Not that she didn't think the men could handle the attack. If anyone could, it was this team of ex-Special Force members. It was just that so much had gone wrong since she stumbled into a murder, any hope in life being balanced between good and bad felt teetered to the side of evil.

The sharp *pop-pop* of gunfire ripped through the air. She wanted to run toward the sound, make sure those she loved were safe, but the Alaskan wilderness was never safe, especially not when it swarmed with snakes not native to its soil. Plus, she'd given her word.

Shouting filled her ear through the com as bullets exploded in rapid succession in the distance. She couldn't make sense of the military commands. Her only comfort was the confidence each voice exuded.

Movement through the dense black spruce limbs caught her eye. She slowly backed further behind the willows, keeping the shadow in her line of vision. Was it an animal startled by the gunfight?

A snap of a branch.

The sharp curse of a man.

Not an animal.

At least, not one of the wild.

Zhang stumbled into a break in the woods. His face twisted in a snarl as his gaze darted behind him. He disappeared back behind the dense branches.

She pressed the mic and whispered, "Davis?"

"Sunny, what's wrong?" Davis's breathless voice answered the instant she let go of the mic button.

"Zhang. He's escaping," she whispered even softer, hoping her words caught the device, but not wanting to alert the man stumbling loudly toward her.

"Stay hidden. I'm coming." The alarm in Davis's voice caught in her throat.

She wouldn't argue. If Zhang's own men were afraid of him, she didn't want to give away her location

Plus, she'd never shot a person.

Just the thought turned sharp in her stomach.

She wasn't even sure she could bluff through holding the vile man at gunpoint, not with her father's constant reminder that one never pointed a gun at something they weren't willing to shoot. Besides, the evil man left a trail a kindergartner could follow. Just in case, though, she unclipped her bear spray, pulled it from its holster, and clicked off the safety.

Zhang fell onto the game trail that followed the creek. The flash of metal on the gun he held in his hand twisted nerves in her gut. Kicking at the root that tripped him, he cussed even louder. When he stood, he yanked something out of his pocket with the hand that didn't hold a gun.

"They think they've won?" He sneered, his face contorting in anger as he looked through the woods toward the gunfire still pinging. "I just need a little more distance, and then they'll see who won."

His laugh pushed vomit up her throat. No. Was he going to blow up the facility?

She had to stop him. She lifted the can of bear spray and waited for him to clear the willows. With her heart's rapid pounding drowning out all other sounds, she prepared to fire.

Chapter Thirty-Two

DAVIS PUSHED through the grappling forest, ignoring the stinging slaps of branches across his face. The thought of Zhang anywhere near Sunny made Davis's mind race with horrible possibilities he didn't want distracting him. Branches snapped behind him as both Rafe and the Rebels followed him.

The gunfire behind them stopped, which wasn't a surprise. The few men at the mine hadn't had a hope against Davis's team. He should have kept a better eye on Zhang. Should have known a man who would send others to kill the opposition would slink out the back while his men fought.

"Davis, he's got a detonator in his hand." Sunny's words yelled through the com, and the angry roar of pain overlapping her voice pushed his legs even faster.

She hadn't stayed hidden.

The loud echo of a single shot and her scream rushed ice through him, causing him to stumble. He caught himself, hot fury burning the cold away, fueling his last push on to the game trail.

Zhang turned this way and that like he couldn't see clearly. His face was bright red from pepper spray. Sunny crawled down the path, clutching her middle with one hand while grabbing for something metal in front of her and chucking it into the forest.

"No," Zhang yelled, lunging for Sunny.

"Zhang," Davis hollered, lifting his gun to take aim.

Zhang grabbed Sunny by the hair, yanked her to her feet, and pulled her to him. Her pain-filled scream had Davis's blood boiling. Zhang turned her around with a gun to her head. Blood soaked Sunny's shirt where she had been shot, making the fabric cling to her belly. Davis's hot anger rushed out in a frigid flurry of torturing images.

"Let her go." Gunnar's low voice growled behind Davis, pulling him back to the present. "You're done. Holding her gets you nowhere."

"It gives me leverage to get free." Zhang's eyes twitched and blinked from the bear spray.

"To where?" Bjørn came up beside Davis, motioning to the trees. "You have no escape. We've disabled your helicopter."

Davis held Sunny's gaze, though the spicy pepper lingering in the air made his eyes, nose, and throat sting. Tears streaked through the dirt on her face. Her dark eyes, usually brimming with hope, held regret and sorrow. He clenched his teeth, ripping his focus from her to the beast keeping her from him.

"I'll figure something out." Zhang's nostrils flared. "I always do. This one survived the wilderness. She'll help me get free."

"I've almost got a shot. Keep him talking." Rafe's voice in Davis's ear hitched hope up his throat.

Sunny's eyes widened, and Davis hated how terrified she must be. He gave her a quick nod of encouragement. Her expression hardened to steeled determination, and pride in the amazing woman she was filled him with the faith he needed to trust. If Rafe needed time, Davis would spin a tale and throw Zhang off kilter.

"You're more of an idiot than I originally thought." Davis goaded, scoffing and lifting his eyebrows as he took a step forward. "You really think she evaded your men? That was me, moron." Davis let the satisfaction at Zhang's ruffled ego lift his mouth. "If you would've done even a minute of research into your neighbor, you'd realize he was ex-military. She's just a hiker, but me? I've got years of Special Forces and military contacts that will take whatever it is you're doing out here and crush it to dust."

Sunny glared at Davis, her eyebrow hitching at Davis's comment, comical in the situation. He'd apologize later. Zhang jerked his arm against her throat, gritting his teeth as he pressed the gun harder against her head. Davis froze, then relaxed his shoulders.

"Almost there," Rafe whispered through the com. "Don't move, Sunny."

"You don't know what you're talking about." Zhang backed up and stumbled, making Sunny whimper in pain. "You haven't crushed anything."

"Maybe." Davis let the fury loose, coating his words with menace. "I do know I will hunt you down, hang you from your ankles in a low hanging tree, and cut you open enough that you won't die, but you'll definitely attract company."

Zhang's throat bobbed, and his eyes darted to the woods surrounding them.

"You callously murdered a good man. Terrorized an innocent woman. Any mercy you deserve, you forfeited when Justin's blood stained the Alaskan soil red," Davis ground out, letting all his anger fill the air.

"Innocent?" Zhang pointed at his red and blotchy face.

"She showed mercy by not shooting you outright," Davis replied.

"Mercy?" Zhang sneered, his muscles bunching.

"Three." Rafe counted as Zhang bared his teeth.

"I don't know the meaning of the word." Zhang tightened his hold on Sunny's throat.

"Two." Rafe continued his count, and Davis held his breath.

"Say goodbye." Zhang smiled at Davis.

"One." Rafe finished.

"Goodbye, Zhang," Sunny choked out.

Zhang's eyebrows scrunched in confusion. Sunny squeezed her eyes closed a second before the report of Rafe's gun shattered the clearing. Zhang's head jerked backward, and he crumbled into a heap, taking Sunny with him. She sobbed and scrambled away.

Davis slid to her side, pulling her onto his lap. "You're okay. It's over."

She collapsed into him, her entire body shaking with adrenaline. He wrapped his arms around her, rocking as the terror of seeing her with the gun to her head eased. He was never letting her out of his sight again.

Bjørn rushed to Zhang's body, while Gunnar scrambled next to Davis. The world collapsed back around Davis. They weren't in the clear yet.

"Let me see." Gunnar grabbed Sunny's shoulder and rolled her from where she clung to Davis.

She kept her hand fisted in the back of his shirt, not letting Gunnar take her out of his arms.

"We need to go, now." Gunnar looked up at Davis, the truth of the severity of the gunshot wound piercing his soul. Gunnar lowered his head back to the injury. "Bjørn?"

"I'm on it." He stood from the dead man and rushed past.

"Wait." Davis called and lifted Sunny enough to dig in his pocket and handed Bjørn the helicopter's spark plugs.

"I'll be ready." Bjørn snatched them, then took off through the woods.

"Let's go." Gunnar reached for Sunny, but Davis waved him off.

With a grunt, he stood with her in his arms. Blood oozed from her and warmed his skin through his clothing. Rafe skidded to a stop as he pushed into the clearing.

"Thanks, man," Davis choked out, clearing the emotion he couldn't let break free. "Thanks for saving her."

Rafe reached over her and pulled Davis's forehead to his. "I've always got your back, brother. Always."

Davis nodded and glanced at Zhang.

"We'll get this cleaned up, then meet you at the hospital." Rafe clapped Davis on the shoulder.

Davis nodded again and rushed back through the woods to the helicopter. Sunny clung to his neck, her face buried against his skin, dampening his collar with tears. If he lost her—he cut off that line of thought and pushed his legs harder. When he broke through the trees to the facility clearing, the Stryker team circled the remaining mine's men at gunpoint. Zeke Greene, Stryker's leader, broke off and ran to Davis's side.

"Make sure Rafe digs deep into what's actually going on here." Davis rushed the words out, though all he wanted to do was focus on Sunny. "There's more here than just mining. And check the binders in the office. Sunny saw something there that needs thorough investigation."

"We'll get it sorted." Zeke squeezed Davis's shoulder. "We've got you."

Davis took a deep breath, inhaling the truth of that statement. "I know. Sorry, I forgot."

"We're family, man. We all get it." Zeke opened his arms to Sunny as they reached the helicopter.

They did. Every single one of them had been through hell and back like Davis had. He swallowed, handed her to Zeke, then climbed into the helicopter.

Zeke handed her back with a nod. "We'll meet up as soon as we get this place cleared."

"Copy," Davis answered as he adjusted his hold on Sunny.

"Lay her here." Gunnar tapped Davis's arm and motioned to a space on the floor between seats.

Though he loathed to let her go, he set her down. She lifted her head, looking down at her saturated shirt, then her gaze darted to him. Her fearful eyes hit him, crushing him like a tank had run him over.

"Davis?" Her voice trembled.

"It's going to be okay. Your brother's the best medic I know." He grabbed her hand and kissed the back of her fingers.

As Bjørn took off, Gunnar grabbed the first-aid kit and pulled her shirt up. Davis's vision blurred at the sight of the bloodied, mangled wound. She went to look, but he jerked his eyes from her stomach and cupped his hands on her cheeks.

"Don't look."

She sucked in a sob, tears racing down her cheeks. "I'm so sorry."

"Shh, it's not your fault."

She grabbed his wrists. "Not yours either."

He shook his head, and she tightened her hold on him.

"Sunny, this is going to hurt." Gunnar's warning jerked her attention away from Davis.

A second later, her scream ripped through the cockpit, then cut off as she passed out. Thank God. Maybe Gunnar could get the worst of it done before she came back around.

"Well?" Davis steeled himself and adjusted his position to help Gunnar.

"I don't know." Gunnar's loud voice broke, and he cleared his throat. "I don't think the bullet hit any major organs, but she's losing a lot of blood, and this kit isn't stocked well."

"I've got freeze-dried plasma on my bird," Bjørn yelled back. "Annie's faster than this heap of junk, anyway."

"Then, we swap helicopters." Gunnar shook his head at the necessary move.

That would waste precious time Sunny might not have. Davis groaned, wrapped his arm around her head, and bent his face down to hers. He let his anguish break free from him, mixing with the tears already drying on her cheeks.

Chapter Thirty-Three

OTIS REDDING PLAYED low from Sunny's phone on the hospital bedside table. Davis had pulled up her playlist hours ago, the music slowly unraveling his nerves. The steady *beep-beep* of her heart monitor had helped more than the music.

He gently squeezed her healing hand laced within his and skimmed the back of his other fingers along the soft skin on the inside of her arm. She sighed, drawing his gaze from his fingers' path to her face. While he wanted her to finally wake up, her eyes remained hidden behind closed lids.

Dark bruises marred beneath her eyes, a testament of the hardships and fight with death she'd fought. He'd almost lost her. Still couldn't believe she'd made it to the hospital, let alone through surgery. Gunnar had used the defibrillator three times between taking off in Bjørn's helicopter and Fairbanks Memorial.

Three times Davis thought the life filled with light he'd barely snagged a glimpse of would disappear to agonizing darkness.

But she'd survived the flight in, her heart flickering like fireflies at night. After hours of surgery, the doctor assured them she'd survive that as well. While the bullet hadn't caused irreparable damage, it had nicked the bottom of her lung, causing a massive loss of blood. If they hadn't switched helicopters and had the medical supplies Bjørn stocked for search and rescue, she'd be dead.

Davis closed his eyes to the sting that thought brought and thanked God she'd survived. Now, Davis would trust the hope stretching before him, a life of him and Sunny taking on adventures together. He bent his head to their hands and kissed her fingers.

The door clicked open, and Davis's muscles bunched. He glanced up as Sunny's mom held the door for her dad, who carried two large takeout bags. Davis's body relaxed, though his stomach twisted with nerves.

"Hey, son. How's our girl doing?" Arne Rebel asked as his eyes scanned his daughter, the "our" settling in Davis's core.

"Still sleeping." He should move, give them time to visit without him hovering, but he couldn't bring himself to let Sunny go.

"Did you get any sleep, hun?" Katie stepped around the bed and pulled Davis in a side hug, patting his shoulder.

"Yeah. I slept." Not much, but enough.

Arne chuckled, the twinkle in his eye telling he knew just how much Davis had slept. Davis shrugged one shoulder and let the corner of his mouth lift into a smile. Katie patted his shoulder again before moving to the bags Arne set on the windowsill. The smoky scent of barbecue overpowered the antiseptic hospital smell and made his stomach growl.

Since the couple had first arrived at the hospital, rushing into the waiting room and pulling Davis into their embraces with tearful thanks, he'd longed to trust the gratitude and acceptance they presented. And so he had, soaking in the love of the Rebel family like he was a desert in a drought. When the doctor had said they could see Sunny, and Katie had grabbed Davis's hand, pulling him into the room with the family, he'd almost lost what little composure he'd had.

Seeing Sunny had shattered it.

He pushed aside the memory of him bawling like a baby and looked at the couple. Katie fussed with pulling containers out of the bags. Arne kept trying to peek, earning a swat from Katie. Man, Davis really hoped they agreed to what he was about to suggest. He cleared his throat, and they both turned in unison.

"I'd like to ask you something." Nervous energy grew thick in his windpipe.

When he didn't continue, Arne lifted an eyebrow. "We're listening."

"You know I hurt Sunny last fall when I didn't contact her." He caught himself fiddling with her hospital bracelet and stopped. "After my last tour, I wasn't in a good place, and though everything in me wanted to follow the blinding light Sunny shone, I was afraid I'd make that light blink out. I was just so paranoid and angry and had little faith in myself or others." He pushed his free hand through his hair, frustrated that he was messing this up. "That probably doesn't make sense."

"Son, I've been there. I know what it's like." Arne

pulled a chair from the wall to the opposite side of Sunny's bed. "How are you now?"

"I came up here to figure that out."

"And did you?" Arne glanced at his wife as she pushed a chair next to him and leaned his forearms across the bed's railing when he peered back at Davis.

"More than I thought I had." His vision blurred as he thought about the last months. "My time away from everyone made me realize just how much they mean to me." He shifted his focus on Sunny's face. "I don't want to waste anymore time second-guessing the love others have for me. Yet, I also know I can't stay at Stryker. I need to be away from that kind of life, always worried about enemy attacks."

"So, what's your plan?" Katie cupped her hands around Sunny's other one resting on the blanket.

"Well—" Davis lifted his mouth in a lopsided grin and looked from Arne to Katie and back again. "Your daughter asked me to marry her, and I'm wanting to as soon as she'll have me."

Katie smiled, her eyes widening. Arne's eyebrows slammed over his. Davis needed to keep talking if he wanted to get both of Sunny's parents on board.

"Then I plan on spending the rest of my life doing everything I can to make her happy and so full of love she bursts. I'm hoping I have your blessings because, with Sunny, my life finally feels whole."

Silence filled the space between them like a bubble about to pop. Or maybe more like the moment a dirty bomb detonates and sound and thought suspends those seconds before the world explodes. Davis held his breath, not sure what he'd say if they disagreed.

"You better say yes or I'm going to be mad." Sunny's

whisper cracked and whipped all three of their gazes to her.

Though her eyelids fluttered tiredly over her eyes, she glared at her dad. She took in a deep breath, then let it out slowly. Davis leaned over her, bringing the back of her fingers to his lips. She turned her dark brown eyes to him.

"I'm not doing another day without Davis, and I need you both to be okay with that." She squeezed his hand, not taking her eyes off him.

"Of course, you have our blessing." Katie's voice shook with tears.

Davis's own face stung with emotion. How could this beautiful woman so full of life love him? It hardly seemed possible. Swallowing the lump in his throat, he pressed a soft kiss to her lips, then sat back up.

"Daddy?" Sunny tore her gaze from Davis to look at her dad.

Davis held his breath.

Arne groaned. "You're pulling the 'daddy' bit?"

Katie scoffed and rolled her eyes.

"You know that's not fair." Arne leaned over and kissed Sunny on the forehead. "I have faith that you and Davis together will make each other stronger versions of yourselves." He sat up and held Davis's stare. "I'll be honored to call him son."

That did it. Davis couldn't hold the tear in that rushed down his cheek. Couldn't form words past the lump in his throat. Arne sniffed, his own eyes glassy, and stretched his hand across the hospital bed. Davis clasped the lifeline offered to him.

"Please tell me that's Big Daddy's barbecue." Sunny's voice broke into the moment, which Davis appreciated since he teetered on bawling like a baby again.

"You know it is." Katie stood and whacked Arne's shoulder. "Help me dish it up."

When they were busy, Davis leaned his elbows on the bed, holding Sunny's hand between his. "So, Sunny Rebel, my Firefly, you want to search out life's adventures together?"

"Yes." She sighed her answer with a smile.

He kissed her knuckles. "When you're out of here, we can start planning."

She shook her head.

"No?"

She eased her hand from his and slid it along his neck. He leaned closer so she didn't have to reach and pull her injuries. He knew how the wrong move could spike pain through a healing gunshot wound.

"No. We start planning today, right after you feed me that smoked brisket Mom is serving up, because the day I get out of this place, I'm marrying you."

Davis closed the distance between them and, with her face cupped in his hands, kissed her. Not as long or as thoroughly as he'd like to. He didn't want to risk the trust her parents had in him.

Chapter Thirty-Four

Sunny turned left, then right in front of her mom's full-length mirror, satisfied that the empire waist and flowing skirt of the wedding dress hid the bulky bandages still covering her wound. In fact, the simple dress, with its crossed satin bust and lace cap sleeves, would have been one she fell in love with even without the need to hide her bandages with the flowing skirt from the bodice. She twisted again and cringed when a sharp pain shot across her abdomen.

"I still can't believe you stumbled on a terrorist group in the middle of nowhere." Sunny's sister, Lena, walked through the door, carrying two bottles of water. "I mean, it's like you're a magnet for trouble."

Sunny gasped. "I'll have you know, trouble rarely finds me. It's the rest of you that can't seem to stay away from it." Come to think of it, it seemed like the Rebel family had a knack for finding danger. "I'm just glad we stopped the plan before it could get past the testing phase. I still can't believe they could've eventually shut down the nation's communication."

"Yeah. I wish I could've been in the Oval Office when the President received *that* report." Lena shook her head. "Rafe calculated the reach of the device mounted to the top of the drill, and all of Alaska's and the Yukon's communication would go dark if they had turned the thing to full capacity. Place two more of those things in the lower forty-eight and all the US is blind."

"Crazy. I'm just glad it's done and don't want to think about it anymore."

Sunny didn't want the nightmare of the attack to darken her wedding day. She rose to her tiptoes and craned to see across the lake to where the ceremony would happen, wondering when they'd be ready for her. Her stitches pulled, and she sucked in a hiss of pain.

"You know, you can wait." Lena's eyes narrowed as she scrutinized Sunny. "The man's had goo-goo eyes for you since you threw yourself at him in the airport back in Kentucky."

"That was acting, you know, to play the part you needed us to so you could whisk your husband away on a honeymoon." Sunny crossed her arms over her chest, careful not to bump her wound. "And he wasn't all goo-goo eyes."

Lena handed Sunny a bottle of water. "I know Davis Fields, and that man was nuts over you from the beginning."

Sunny's cheeks warmed at the declaration.

"Which makes me know for a fact that he's not going anywhere." Lena set her bottle on their mom's dresser lined with pictures of the family growing up. "You can wait, heal up completely, get to know each other outside of a stressful situation."

Sunny huffed a laugh. That was the understatement of the year. Lena took Sunny's bottle, set it down, then grabbed both her hands. Sunny's eyes widened. She couldn't remember the last time Lena let down her tough-as-nails exterior. Had marriage softened her, made her less intimidating?

"You don't have to worry that he's going to disappear on you," Lena said, her voice soft and caring.

She squeezed Sunny's hands, making her nose and eyes tingle. Shoot. She blinked to keep the tears at bay. She'd actually put on make-up, and, even though it was waterproof, she didn't want to risk it running down her face.

"Besides, if he did, he knows I'll track him to the ends of the world and make him pay in slow, agonizing torture for hurting you." And there was the Lena Sunny loved.

Sunny laughed, gingerly pulling her sister into a hug. "Thanks, Lena, but I'm not marrying him now because I'm worried he'll leave. I'm marrying him because I can't spend another day apart from him."

She stepped back and shrugged, looking out the window toward the lake. The clear, forget-me-not blue sky promised a beautiful, dry day. The rains the week before had filled the stretch of land between her parents' cabin and the jutting Alaska Range beyond with wildflowers. She always imagined she'd get married on the top of some mountain somewhere, but now she realized just how perfect having the ceremony here, where love had raised her, would be. Her face hurt with the width of her smile as she turned back to Lena.

"If my siblings and the last year have taught me anything, it's that life is short." Sunny had watched the heartache Lena had lived through when her first fiancé, Ethan, had died and how Gunnar had put happiness on hold, thinking he could either have duty or love, but not both. "I want to spend every moment I can being Mrs. Sunniva Fields."

"Good, because it's time for you to get a move on." Tiikâan strutted into the room.

Sunny squealed and rushed to him. "I didn't think you were going to make it!"

His embrace, while tight, wrapped around her carefully. So, someone had updated him on her status. She smirked. No secrets in her family.

Lena patted her shoulder as she left. "See you out there."

"So, baby sis, you're really ready to tie the knot?" Tiikâan stepped back, his gaze scanning her face.

"Absolutely." Sunny beamed at him, bouncing on her toes. "How are you even here? I thought you weren't going to be able to get away."

His cheek flexed and eyes hardened before he curtained whatever bothered him with a smile. "I convinced the boss lady she could survive without me for a day." He glanced at his watch. "But we'll have to get this ceremony on a roll if I'm going to see you get married."

"You can't stay?"

"I've only got an hour before I have to head back to the disaster I've gotten myself into."

"Is it that bad? I thought you were just flying people back and forth to the work site."

"It's fine." He tucked her hand into the crook of his arm. "Let's just say guiding hunters is a lot less drama than corporate execs, but the money is going to set me up to expand my guiding business exactly like I want to."

Sunny swallowed away the disappointment. "Well, I'm glad you could make it, even if it's for a short while."

"Me too." He led her outside to the canoe waiting at the dock.

Her mother had filled the inside with flowers, leaving just the space for her and Tiikâan open. He helped her get settled onto the bench, then pushed off from the dock. Sunny's heart pounded in her chest, her palms sweating. She tried to let the fragrance of the flowers and the steady splash of the oars calm her, but it didn't help.

Scanning the small crowd of people waiting on the other side of the lake, she couldn't find Davis. Her siblings waited on the left of the willow arch her dad and brothers had thatched together. Davis's friends from the Stryker team lined the right side of the arch, but her parents blocked Davis as they stood before him.

Were they warning him? Threatening him with life and limb if he hurt her? That would be just like Dad. She bunched her fists in her dress, then quickly smoothed it out.

Her mom pulled Davis into a hug, and Dad followed suit. When they stepped away, they both brushed their hands across their cheeks. Oh, dear. Before Sunny could worry too much over their tears, her eyes caught Davis's.

He took a step forward, stopping when Rafe's hand clamped over his shoulder. Sunny thought there was laughter, but her pulse pounded so loud in her ears, it was all she heard. Everything else blurred until all she saw was Davis.

Dad helped her out of the boat, and she fairly floated toward her future. Tears streaked Davis's cheeks, and he dashed them away. She licked her lips and tasted salt. When had she started crying?

Her dad answered the pastor's question about who gave her away and handed her to Davis. Before he turned her to the pastor, he stepped close. His hands squeezed hers.

"Thank you for finding me in my darkness, Firefly." He kissed her, the laughter of those watching hitting her ears and making her smile.

"Hey," Bjørn hollered from behind her. "Save that for the end."

"Sorry." Davis's smirk was anything but repentant.

"Well, then—" Pastor Jerry cleared his throat, his eyes sparkling with mirth. "Dearly, beloved."

Sunny held Davis's gaze the entire ceremony, her vows breathless as they pushed past her tight throat. She never imagined she'd trust again, never imagined the loneliness that had weighed her down would be nothing but a wisp of memory. Yet, in her darkest moment, love had found her and led her home.

Epilogue

TIIKÂAN GLANCED at his watch for what seemed like the hundredth time since he'd arrived at his parents' place two hours earlier. Laughter pulled his attention back to the bride and groom as they danced to one of Sunny's old songs from the 50s on the makeshift dance floor Dad and his brothers had built. As much as he wanted to stay, especially since all his family had made it, he had to get going.

He scanned the yard, still surprised his brother Magnus had been able to leave the forest fire he fought by Denali and that their sister Astryde had taken time away from her busiest commercial fishing season. Though, the way she hustled, *every* season was her busiest. Tiikâan heaved a sigh and headed to his parents talking with Bjørn and his fiancée, Sadie.

"I've got to get back to the North Slope." Tiikâan pulled his mom into a hug.

"So soon?" She held him tight.

"Yeah." He kissed her on the top of the head and let go to hug Sadie and shake Bjørn's hand. "I promised I'd be there to take the boss lady back to Barrow this evening."

His promise had been what had finally got his boss, Merritt, to relent and let him leave. Well, that and his threat to quit. She'd already been through three other pilots, and he'd banked on the fact that she couldn't afford anymore delays.

"The job going okay?" Dad shook Tiikâan's hand and pulled him into a crushing hug.

"Eh, it's all right."

He didn't want to elaborate and have his family worry. They'd just gone through hell and back with Sunny's disappearance and brush with death. Him telling them about the trouble the work site was dealing with would just make them anxious all over again.

Besides, he was just a glorified taxi in the air and polar bear guard. None of the drama the company was dealing with while cleaning up the gas spill had to affect him. He'd just keep his head down, fly Merritt back and forth to the spill site, keep alert to any bears wandering close, and make the bankroll necessary to get his hunting and guiding business to the next level. Just a few more months and he'd be set.

A text dinged on his phone as he crossed the field to his airplane. He waved one last time to his family as he pulled his phone from his pocket. His steps stalled to a halt at the words.

MERRITT: I NEED TO TALK TO YOU IN PRIVATE WHEN YOU GET BACK. I NEED HELP, AND I DON'T KNOW WHO ELSE TO TRUST.

What could she possibly need Tiikâan's help with? He knew next to nothing about drilling. Her stress that had filled his small plane so thick he'd pushed his plane to fly faster hadn't eased in the weeks he'd been flying her. If anything, it'd gotten worse.

He typed her a quick response that he was on his way and sprinted to his plane. If there was something he could do to help, he'd do it. He just hoped it was enough.

Pre-order A Rebel's Shot from the author and get your copy before anywhere else. Visit www.sarablackard.com to order and get all the latest book news.

Also by Sara Blackard

Vestige in Time Series
Vestige of Power
Vestige of Hope
Vestige of Legacy
Vestige of Courage

Stryker Security Force Series
Mission Out of Control
Falling For Zeke
Capturing Sosimo
Celebrating Tina
Crashing Into Jake
Discovering Rafe
Convincing Derrick
Honoring Lena

Alaskan Rebels Series
A Rebel's Heart
A Rebel's Beacon
A Rebel's Promise
A Rebel's Trust

Wild Hearts of Alaska

Wild About Denali

Wild About Violet

Wild About Rory

Other Books

Meeting Up with the Consultant

About the Author

Sara Blackard has been a writer since she was able to hold a pencil. When she's not crafting wild adventures and sweet romances, she's homeschooling her five children, keeping their off-grid house running, or enjoying the Alaskan lifestyle she and her husband love.